The Crying Willows

MASON LAKEY

ISBN 978-1-63874-789-5 (paperback)
ISBN 978-1-63874-791-8 (hardcover)
ISBN 978-1-63874-790-1 (digital)

Copyright © 2021 by Mason Lakey

All rights reserved. No part of this publication may be reproduced, distributed, or transmitted in any form or by any means, including photocopying, recording, or other electronic or mechanical methods without the prior written permission of the publisher. For permission requests, solicit the publisher via the address below.

Christian Faith Publishing, Inc.
832 Park Avenue
Meadville, PA 16335
www.christianfaithpublishing.com

Printed in the United States of America

ACKNOWLEDGMENTS

I want to thank God for giving me the talent to write. Thank you to all who helped with book signings: Rebecca, Elaine, and Nancy. A special thanks to my friend Linda for reminding me to update my book and put in it my love of nature.

CHAPTER 1

The Crying Willows

I was sitting in my favorite chair watching a net flick when my cell rang. It was Andy Duncan, my agent. He and I had been working on an idea for my next book, one about a wealthy family who had made it big in small town USA. In his excited voice, he said, "Angie, I have found the perfect town, the perfect family, and the perfect setting for your new book."

When I hung up, I wondered why I had agreed. However, I did need to get a new book underway. It would only take about three months to get the feel of the place and of the family, now and fifty years ago.

It suddenly hit me that I had to get up and get busy. I had to start packing. I would have to let Jack know where I was going.

Jack was a handyman Mom and I employed to help us around the house with yard work. I always liked Jack to know where to reach me, in case anything happened to the house or he needed to do some work while I was gone.

I would call Mom and let her know I would be gone for a few months. Mom and Jack had a key, and between the two of them, they could look after things for me.

I took the rest of the week getting ready to leave for my new adventure in Charlottesville, Virginia. Andy Duncan would meet me in Charlottesville a week from Monday. I phoned the airlines and got the schedule for my flight. I phoned Mom and Jack to let them know I would be leaving the airport in Kentucky at 7:00 a.m. and would arrive in Virginia about 7:45 a.m. on Monday morning. Well, everything was set for my leaving. Now I must work on getting some rest for my leaving between this Sunday and the next.

I went to bed early on Sunday night and watched a net flick, an old movie. I fell asleep rather quickly. I slept on Monday. When I finally made myself get up and put on the coffee, my doorbell rang. I threw on my robe. Standing outside my door was Mom. She said, "I just thought you would need a hand."

Before she could finish, I said, "I have everything under control. Everything is done except cleaning the apartment, and I can manage."

"Oh no, young lady," she said, "I'll help."

I saw there was no stopping her, so I said, "All right. Sit down first and let's have some coffee." She did, and we talked a bit, then it was straight to cleaning. We finally finished around 1:00 p.m., getting everything out of the refrigerator and cleaning closets and all the things I did not tend to every day.

Mom and I decided to get something to eat. We went to a Chinese restaurant close by.

I ate too much, as usual. Mom and I made plans to go to the mall the next day and do some shopping. Afterward, I dropped Mom off at the country house and headed back to my apartment in town.

On my way back into town, I was thinking how nice it would be to be a housewife. Mom was always bragging to her friends about me. She would say how proud she was of me. She didn't know how much I would give to trade places with her at times. Well, enough of that kind of thinking. I did not need to depress myself before going on my journey. It was just that ever since Luke and I had broken our engagement, I felt I needed someone special in my life.

As I opened the door to my apartment, the phone was ringing. It was Andy. He was already in Charlottesville and had booked a hotel for us. His room would be just down the hall so we could work together for the first week. He would then go back home, leaving me to the task at hand.

When I arrived in Charlottesville on Monday, I went straight to my room, telling Andy I would meet him for dinner. My hotel room was comfortable and clean, my two must-haves.

THE CRYING WILLOWS

I always dreaded the first two or three days, knowing I would be unable to sleep for at least that long. I got out my pen and pad to take notes on the people I would be meeting the next day.

When I arrived at the dining room, Andy was already seated. I took out my pad and pen and began to write about the people who were to be the subject of the autobiography. We had dinner as I wrote. I just had a Greek salad and some tea.

The people I would be writing about were the Tuckerings, a very distinctive family who had a huge corporation in Richmond. For the past fifty years, they had been a major exporter of clothing and materials and had several shops around town that sold their clothing. They owned most of the stores in the mall—Tuck's, TJ's, and Johnese's.

Johnese was the only daughter of John Tuckering Jr. Mr. John Tuckering Sr., the founder of the company, was Johnese's grandfather. He had died twenty years before. John Junior, Johnese's father, was now CEO of the company, and Johnese was his right arm. The word was that without all of Johnese's designs, this company would not be so stable. Danese, John's sister, had a great business sense, but she did not have a flair for design.

I wrote down questions, such as when the company first began and how financially stable it was. All those boring details would be over, and I could move on.

CHAPTER 2

The Tuckering Estate

Mr. Tuckering and Johnese were supposed to meet with me the next day at their wonderful estate. I was quite intrigued to learn how the richer half lived. It was supposed to be a grand place. I would find out the next day.

The next morning, I was very excited. I couldn't wait to see what a beautiful place this must be. I sat down and had a cup of coffee, and by the time I was finished, Andy was ready to go.

We departed via a nice limousine, compliments of the Tuckerings. We drove out of town about fifteen miles. The road became very curvy. There were splendid rolling hills all around, and lots of beautiful trees along the way. The estate was all I had hoped for. If a writer couldn't write here, she couldn't write anywhere.

We entered the gate and went up what seemed to be the longest winding driveway I'd ever seen. Along the driveway, sturdy oak and maple trees graced either side. The setting was so glorious.

Then I saw it for the first time: an impressively grand house, large enough for my entire apartment building three times over! It was a huge stucco house. The setting was an old English country home. It was, however, called a châteauesque-style house from the gilded age. The sidewalk up to the house was quite a long walk. We went onto the enormous porch and rang the doorbell. A lady opened the door. Her name was Heidi, so her name tag said. She led us into a grand hall with two large rooms on either side. Heidi ushered us into the room on the left. It was what I supposed would be called a sitting room. It had a French door with a Roman arch at the top. It led out onto a patio that I imagined would be quite nice in spring.

The furniture and paintings in the room looked as if they had come out of the antique shop or art gallery. Of course, I knew nothing of antiques or art, so I wouldn't know if that were true, but judging by the house, I supposed it was so.

Heidi returned with John Junior and Johnese. Both of them welcomed us graciously and invited us to have tea with them in the sitting room. We graciously accepted their invitation. I felt like a queen; it was wonderful. I talked with the Tuckerings about their business and lives in general. John Junior told me how his father had been a poor man and how he made it big in materials before later expanding to design.

"What happened to your father?" I asked.

"He had a sudden death twenty years ago."

Well, that told me nothing, but I decided not to pry, so I asked nothing else.

I talked with Johnese. She was very interesting; a real go-getter, I could tell. She showed me some of her designs. I could see why she was so famous. They were amazing. When another lady came into the room, Mr. Tuckering introduced her as Danese Tuckering, his sister. She just didn't seem to fit in somehow. She was elegant enough, but there was just something about her, something I could not quite put my finger on. We chatted for a while, and I thanked them for inviting me into their home. I started to leave, and John Tuckering said, "Oh no, we hoped you would stay here with us. It would be much easier for you."

I said, "I really don't want to impose."

"Not at all," he replied. "I insist."

"Well, I suppose we can try that," I agreed.

At this point, Heidi came and showed me to the room where I would be staying. We went up the winding stairs to the second floor, following the hallway to the end. The room was exquisite, as big as my apartment, with a king-sized bed and a balcony that looked out over the garden. Beyond the garden, I could see a row of willow trees. I knew I would most definitely be more comfortable here than at the hotel, even if I didn't sleep the first night or two. Heidi gave Andy and me a tour of the house. It was just amazing. The only thing I was thinking while she was showing us around was that I would have to stay in my room a lot in order to not get lost. I would be fine with using the library, the dining room, and, of course, this lovely bedroom.

Andy went back into town that afternoon. I sat in the library, gathering information about the family, such as from where they originated, when the first John Tuckering was married, and what happened to the first Mrs. Tuckering. As it turned out, they had separated when young John was only two years old.

Oddly enough, Mr. Tuckering had gotten custody of the young children. I found that strange, because at that time, it was not a common thing for fathers to have custody and for mothers to have visitation rights. It struck me as very odd.

While talking to Heidi, I found out that the business was started two years before John was born. That made John Junior forty-eight years old. He certainly did not look it. He was a very handsome man. The senior Mr. Tuckering was only married ten years and never remarried. Most young men would have remarried at some point, but he did not.

Johnese was twenty and just out of school, full of life and ambition. I always loved to see freshness and the desire to achieve. It is something I had been lacking of late, or so I thought. Mom did not think so, of course. She thought I had no flaws.

I finished my work in the library that day. Mom was calling me, wanting to know about everything. She had so many questions I sometimes thought she should have been the writer.

I started to wind down for the night. Before I turned in, I decided to step out on the balcony and enjoy the nice breeze blowing. I heard something that sounded as if it were a cry, soft and low, a sad sound. In a way, though, it was not sad at all. It was a low, soft whispering sound.

About that time, Heidi knocked on the door of my room. I opened it, and she handed me some hot tea. "It will help you sleep," she said, and I thanked her. "You have heard them, haven't you?" she asked.

"Heard what?"

"The crying willows," she replied.

"Yes, I believe I did. Why are they called the crying willows?"

THE CRYING WILLOWS

"That is a long story," she answered. "Someday, I will tell you. Sleep now. Goodnight."

Heidi was sort of a strange lady, I thought. She went with the house, so to speak. She was a bit stuffy, but she emitted an inner beauty.

The crying willows—what a great title. Oh, well. I drank my nice warm tea and went to bed, falling asleep rather quickly, to my surprise.

The morning brought a beautiful autumn day, and the landscaping from the balcony was quite breathtaking. The rose garden on the left side was magnificent. Looking toward the back of the house, it was as if you could see for miles, with those wonderfully impressive willows at the very back.

The earth seemed to be saying, *I need a rest*. The leaves were falling from the trees and whirling all around. I could see some little squirrels scampering around, working hard to put all their nuts away for winter. Most people love spring or summer. However, autumn has always been my most favorite time of the year, a time to get ready to rest and replenish and bring about a beautiful new time of year. There was a colorful lunar moth sitting on my windowsill with its wings spread. The gorgeous green wings and yellow circles looked as though you could see right through them. This would be my last look at the lunar moth, as upon further investigation, it was not alive; but it was beautiful.

I rushed about to get ready, and when I finally got started, I saw Danese walking a dog. I went out the door just as they happened by. "Is this your dog, Danese?" I asked.

"Yes, this is Sadie," she replied.

"Well, she is beautiful."

"Thank you," she said. "She is a great dog."

I grabbed my smartphone. With my voice recorder on it, I was off to Johnese's office this morning to see firsthand how a successful dress designer spent her day, or what was left of the day. These were the times I really was glad to be a writer. I could set my own schedule. I kept thinking about Danese and her dog. It just seemed out of character for her. Sadie was a Siberian husky, a spectacular specimen of a dog.

I entered the building, telling the security guard who I was and that I had an appointment with Johnese. He directed me to the elevator and informed me that Johnese's office was on the fourth floor and that she was expecting me.

I could not help but notice the beautiful designs. She certainly was in the right business! When I got to the fourth floor, I was greeted by a secretary. I told her who I was, and she said Johnese's office was at the end of the hall. I tapped on the door. Upon opening it, Johnese and her father, John, were arguing. When they saw me, I said, "I'm sorry. Have I come at a bad time?"

"Oh no, it's a wonderful time," Johnese said. "My dad was just leaving."

"Miss Larimore, I'll see you at another time. If I can be of any assistance to you, let me know. My office is at the other end of the hall," John said courteously.

"Thank you, Mr. Tuckering." I replied.

When he was gone, Johnese said, "Don't mind him. We argue about everything—materials, colors, designs. I think we would argue, even if we both liked the product, about which of us liked it most. I suppose that is because we are so much alike. May I call you Angie? You are not here to hear about my dad's and my arguments. What would you like to know?"

"Actually," I said, "I would like to tag along with you and go through your day—well, what is left of it. I'll take notes, record what you do, and just listen, if you don't mind. I admire your work very much. Where did you develop such a talent?"

"From my dad, I suppose," Johnese replied, "besides growing up in a world of fabrics, patterns, and colors. My dad made sure I went to one of the best schools in the world."

"I won't trouble you anymore with my chatter," I told her. "I will just observe until lunch. After that, I will bother your dad, if he will allow me to do so."

The day went very quickly for me. I enjoyed watching them lay out materials and cutting fabrics on the cutting table before they were sewn and inspected. Johnese and John had to approve them.

Then the label would go on, then the price tag, then they were sent to be packed and shipped all over the world.

The day went so quickly that I asked if I could spend the entire week as I had done that day. John and Johnese seemed to have no objections.

At dinner that evening, I met with Andy and told him all about things I had learned. "I think this will be a very interesting story," I told Andy. "I think you did it this time, Andy. You have picked a subject matter I will thoroughly enjoy."

Andy and I had a good dinner. I could tell he was getting restless. I asked him to stay until the end of the week, and we could then correspond by e-mail and phone. He agreed. I planned to start my manuscript after the next evening. I was going to talk with John about the early days of his company. I wanted to touch on the company in the generation before his. I promised Andy he could see a rough draft of a chapter or two by then, and he was satisfied with that.

We finished dinner, and Andy drove me back to the estate. The next day, I needed to rent a car. I am a terrible procrastinator. I had to do that the next day.

I went straight to my room, not wanting to linger, as I was anxious to work on my notes. I worked until around midnight. I went onto the balcony, this being my favorite spot already. It seemed as though you were escaping the entire world there. The willows were crying in the wind, a phenomenal sound. It was a peaceful time, but I went quickly inside when a big gust of wind reached me.

CHAPTER 3

Designs by Johnese

The morning brought me to a rude awakening. I had promised myself I would be a real working lady that day. I got up at 6:00 a.m. Normally, I didn't realize there was such a time. I dressed and caught a ride into town with John, promising I would rent a car that day.

We arrived at the office at 8:00 a.m., and my day began, making notes and taping bits and pieces of interesting things. Things that were ordinary to them were quite out of the ordinary to me. I took pictures with my phone of the packing, shipping, and how things were handled. It was quite amazing to me. Right where I was, the designs I saw being made that day would be all over the world in a day or so. I spent the biggest part of my day with cutters, seamstresses, inspectors, packers, and the shipping department. It all fascinated me.

I arranged a meeting with John that afternoon to talk about the company from the time he took it over. John talked about his town, his work, and his family. I thanked him for his time and patience with me and promised to leave him alone after the next day. I went up to my room a little early, as I really needed to get some work done on my manuscript. I was pleased with what I had done so far. It would be ready for Andy at the end of the week, at least two chapters in rough draft. Then he and I could fight over what I would not change.

John Tuckering was strictly a businessman. Although he spoke with pride about his daughter, I wondered how much communication there was between them. John was very busy, and the business was just about the only thing that was talked about at home or anywhere.

I spent the next day reading about the senior John Tuckering. The book in the library told me that John Senior was of Irish background. His family had immigrated to the USA in the late 1800s. He was raised poor, started the company from nothing, beginning by peddling his things from door-to-door. He made enough money to expand, and the company began to grow. He worked very hard. Now his company was one of the largest in the world.

I wondered why this was the place he chose to settle. Maybe it was the climate. It was mild here but there was some snow in the winter.

When I had compiled all of the information about Mr. Tuckering Senior, I thought it was time to touch base with John Junior. I caught up with him just after lunch to ask about the personal side of Mr. Tuckering Senior. John said, "Well, there's not a lot to tell. My father worked very hard, day and night, to build this company. We all owe him a great debt. He died at a young age."

"How did your father die?" I asked.

"He died in an accident. Miss Larimore, I am sorry. Could we continue at another time?"

"Certainly, Mr. Tuckering," I replied.

"I have some things to attend to."

I felt as if he did not want to talk about his father's death.

CHAPTER 4

Danese

Danese Tuckering was a quiet, reserved lady, not at all like her brother, John. John Junior was strictly business, but I would guess that all of Johnese's drive came from him.

Danese was very lovely, tall and thin with copper red hair and beautiful brown eyes. I asked her if I could meet with her the following day, and after checking her calendar, she agreed to give me the afternoon.

Danese was a businesswoman, much more introverted than John. I thought how nice it must be to be able to work with your family. Danese was very nice, but there was something different about her. She seemed incredibly fond of Sadie, her Siberian husky, as if she was trying to replace something in her life. That seemed a bit peculiar to me.

I finally rented a car. I took myself to a few of the shops around town that afternoon, looking for Johnese's designs. I didn't have to look very far—they were everywhere. It was as if this entire town depended on this company. I bought Mom a sweater that looked perfect for her. When I arrived back at the house that evening, I went straight to my room to get started on my book.

I started the first chapter, then stopped abruptly, seeing that I would have to spend a little more time in the library or with John Tuckering. I really did not have enough background on the senior Mr. Tuckering. I needed to know about the accident, but I did not feel at all comfortable about asking John Mr. He seemed as though he did not want to talk about it.

I took a break from writing and went onto the balcony once again. It was as if it called to me. I heard the willows blowing in the wind. The crying of the willows was not a sad sound to me, but rather soothing. I sat there for quite a while, listening to the wind in the willows and watching two deer playing in the field. They played like children. How nice it must be to be so free! I finally went to bed around 11:00 p.m.

The next morning, I slept until 9:00 a.m. and was just getting out of bed when there was a knock at my door. I grabbed my robe and opened the door, and there was Heidi with my breakfast. I thanked her but told her it was not necessary as I was not a breakfast person. She asked if I would be dining with them that night, and I told her I would not as I had to talk with Andy that evening.

I was standing out on the balcony when I noticed Danese and her dog getting into a white convertible and driving away. I wondered where they were going. I went down to the library. I was so glad to have such a marvelous library right there in the house. I was looking to see if I could find anything from twenty years before.

I spent all morning in the library but found nothing about the accident. There was plenty of news about John Senior—when he opened the plant, when the construction of the office began—but nothing about the accident at all.

I had to get to the office meeting with Danese. When I arrived at the office, I gave the secretary in the lobby my name and who I wanted to see. She told me to go on in. I walked straight through the big doors. Danese's office was in front of me. I tapped at the door. As I opened it, I noticed that the office was like Danese, very clean and neat.

"What may I tell you, Angie? May I call you Angie?"

"Certainly. I seem to be having a hard time getting the feel of the past generation, about your father and how different things were."

"Oh, they were very different. My father worked very hard to start the company. Our mother never worked, but she supported my father's work, doing anything to make it easier."

"Could you tell me about the early years?" I asked.

"Yes. As a matter of fact, I brought a scrapbook for you, if you would like to study it. It has pictures and a lot of facts and figures."

"All right. I will take it with me, if that is okay. When your father died, how old were you and John?"

"Well, John was twenty-eight and I was thirty-two."

It surprised me that she was older than John. She didn't look to be fifty-two years old.

"I also wanted to ask you about John Junior's wife."

"She died when Johnese was born, and he never married again. I had hoped he would. Instead, he tied himself up with work, and that is basically the story."

"How did your father die?" I asked.

"In a horrible accident," she replied stiffly. "We never discuss it."

"Well, thank you for your time. I do appreciate it."

"Good luck with your book, Angie. We want you to do well. We could use the publicity."

I talked with Andy over the phone that evening and told him I needed more information about John Senior's death to do a correct biography on the family. He said he would help me search on the following day. After I hung up the phone, I worked for about three hours and quit early. I thought I had a decent start, but I decided to go down to the library in the house to see if there might be anything there of interest.

I also had to go through the scrapbook that Danese had given me. I was looking through some design books from the early years when a picture fell to the floor. I picked it up and couldn't believe my eyes. There was a picture of the Tuckering family. Mr. Tuckering Senior bore quite a striking resemblance to John, and there was a beautiful woman who looked very much like Danese. There were three children in the picture. John looked to be about a year old, Danese about four or five, and another child who looked exactly like Danese. On the back of the picture, all it said was *The Tuckerings*.

I put the picture back and thought no more of it. About that time, John came into the library, and I talked with him about the early designs and how they had changed. John would talk about business all night, but not about personal things. John was such a handsome man with all that gorgeous black hair. I just couldn't understand why he was not married. I felt a little pull toward John and thought he could be very pleasant if he would just let his guard down. He would talk about his daughter. He was so proud of her and her accomplishments.

I said good evening to John. I really wanted to stay and talk with him, but in the back of my mind, I kept wondering about the picture. I finally dismissed it and went to bed.

The morning brought a beautiful day. It was not cold, but there was a nip in the morning air to remind us that it was fall.

While I was walking around the property, I spotted a young deer reaching up to the apple tree to have a little snack. I watched for a few minutes. I couldn't imagine living anywhere without all this glorious wildlife. I went back into the house. Johnese was ready to go out as usual. John and Danese were a little lackadaisical that morning, as I was every morning. We were having our last coffee when I asked casually, "Just how many were in your family, John?"

"What do you mean?" He looked startled.

"Was it just you and Danese?"

"Oh. Yes, of course," he replied.

"John and I were the only children," Danese said, "and our father never married again. I'm going to rest for a while."

"All right, Danese," replied John, "but don't be very long."

"I won't, John," she said and went up the stairs.

"Angie, will you be going with us this morning?" John asked.

"Not this morning, John."

"That's our loss," John replied and smiled. I had really never seen John smile before. It was very pleasant.

I thought Danese had looked very pale, and I asked John if she was all right. He answered, "Yes. Thank you for your concern. She just gets overly tired sometimes. I will see you this evening."

I went straight to my room and started work. I was working rather intently when the phone rang. I didn't answer it at first until I realized I was in the house alone. Heidi was off that day, and apparently Danese was already gone.

"Tuckering residence."

"Hello, dear. Are you the young writer?"

"Yes, ma'am." I replied.

"Well, if you want to know the true story about the Tuckerings, come and see me. I am Mrs. Greenbrier, and I live at 242 Emerson Way, just two blocks up from you. Come today. You will not regret coming." Then she was gone.

This story was getting stranger and stranger all the time, I thought. I wondered what skeletons were in the closet. Being a writer, I had to check it out. I called Mom to see if she had received her sweater. I told her Andy had returned the week before, and I would be taking a break in about two weeks. We hung up and I decided I would find 242 Emerson Way. So off I went.

CHAPTER 5

Mrs. Greenbrier

As I drove to Mrs. Greenbrier's house, I thought how lovely these French country homes were. They all had wonderful rose gardens somewhere on their properties. I rang the bell and identified myself at the intercom. The gate opened. The drive all the way up to the house was bordered on each side with what would surely be beautiful flowering trees in the spring.

The house was fantastic, an enormous stucco house with a porch from side to side and huge white columns all along the front. I rang the bell, and a maid answered the door. She took me to a wonderful room at the end of the hall where an elderly gray-haired lady was sitting. Mrs. Greenbrier. By looking at her, I thought she might be more than seventy. She was sitting with a shawl around her shoulders.

The lady turned to me and said, "Please sit down and listen to me. I hope you will believe me. Not many other people do. When I am gone, no one will know the truth about the Tuckerings."

I sat, and she said, "I knew John Senior and his wife and their children. My husband and I never had children, and I adored theirs. We would go to their house and they came to ours. No one ever visited them except us. I babysat for them. They had three children."

"But," I interjected, "I thought there were only two."

"That is what everyone thought, but there was another girl, a twin to Danese. Her name was Janese. They never took her out of the house. She was a little slow. I don't know that they were ashamed of her. Maybe they thought it was for her own good. Anyway, she had to stay in the house. She was allowed to go into the garden out back and play where no one could see her. When the children were little, they would take John and Danese, but not Janese. Janese was a wonderful, sweet little girl most of the time, but she could be incorrigible at times. I think she was too much for Mrs. Tuckering to handle by herself.

"One night, Janese took such a fit that Mrs. Tuckering said she could not raise a child like that, and she left John. John Junior was only two, and the girls were five. I suppose John thought it would be too much for him, with work being so demanding, so he put Janese into a home for the handicapped. When she was around twenty-five, John Junior and Danese followed their father one night and found out where she was staying. They confronted their father and demanded that he bring Janese home, but he refused.

"When Janese was around thirty, there was a fire at the home where she was staying. It changed operators after that, and the law had changed, so Janese was no longer allowed to live there. John and Danese were so excited. They thought they could help their sister get well.

"For two years, Janese stayed at the estate, and Danese just took over her care. She taught Janese things that no one thought she was capable of learning. Twins always have a special bond.

"To make a long story short, one night she went crazy, killing her father with a gun. Well, that is the way the story goes, anyway. They were all beside themselves. They called and asked if they could bring Janese to me, but I didn't know why until the next day. No one knew about Janese, so they called the police and told them their father was cleaning his gun and it went off. No one questioned their word, and until this day, everyone thinks it was an accident. The next day, Janese was taken away, but I don't know where. I do know John and Danese go to see her. So you can tell their story, or you can find the real one. It's up to you."

Mrs. Greenbrier gave me a lot of newspaper clippings. I took them, thanked her, and left. She was an old lady. Maybe she didn't know what she was talking about or was just mixed up. Still, there was that picture. I had my work cut out for me now.

CHAPTER 6

Heidi

I went back to the estate, more confused than ever. I went straight to the library and found the picture I had seen there, slipping it into my pocket. I read for a while, then went up to my room. I was looking at the scrapbook that Danese had given me. There were lots of photos here, but none of them included another child.

Heidi knocked at my door and asked if I had a moment to talk with her. I agreed, thinking to myself that nothing else I could hear today could shock me now.

Heidi, being the kind of person she was, did not know how to relax or talk to people. It was as if she was trying to get something off her chest. She started by saying, "I am going to tell you things that will seem strange, and mind you, I don't even know if they are true. This story has been told in these parts for years. You see, some folks believe that John Tuckering Sr. was not killed by accident. Some think that John Junior did it to get the old man's money. I don't think that, though. John is not that kind of man. He's not that coldhearted. I'll tell you what I think. I think it was Danese. John, of course, would cover for her.

"The story goes that one night, a gunshot was heard at the Tuckerings around midnight, but the police were not called until an hour later. Ever since that night, Danese has acted strange, very strange. That is when the willows started to cry. Folks around here think that until the murder is solved, the willows will continue to cry. Well, you are the one."

"The one for what, Heidi?" I asked.

"The one come to help us solve this murder."

"I am a writer, not a detective!" I said.

"You must do this, Angie. It is your destiny," Heidi declared, then left as abruptly as she had come.

I sat there, almost numb. This was getting crazy. Mrs. Greenbrier told me about a child who may or may not exist. Heidi told me that the father was killed by Danese, but everyone thinks John did it. I decided what I would do. Very early the next day, I would take a nice long walk, put on a net flick—a comedy—and clear my head before giving any more thought to this.

I went out into the garden for a while. I imagined that in spring, the garden must be very beautiful. It looked as though there were at least a half dozen different types of roses here. I walked toward the edge of the garden, and much to my surprise, found an absolutely stunning view of the mountains and a wonderful bench to sit upon. So that was where I spent my afternoon. I watched as a lazy little turtle made its way across the yard.

At dinner, I announced I would be leaving for two weeks before returning. I thanked them for being so kind to me.

CHAPTER 7

My Trip Home

I returned to my room and called Mom to let her know I would be visiting. I hung up and packed my things for the trip, then got my writing in order. I called Andy to let him know I was coming home and would meet him in a couple of days.

My thoughts, however, were not on the trip but on all the things I had heard. Should I explore it at all, or should I tell Andy? With questions but no answers, I went to bed early. I slept quite well and awoke around 6:00 a.m. I couldn't believe I had awoken so early, so I decided to go down for breakfast.

When I was walking down the stairs, I heard Johnese going out the door. When she had closed the door, Danese called out to John and went into the dining room. I paused as I was about to proceed into the dining room and could hear Danese talking to John. She seemed very worried about something. The only thing I could make out was that John wanted Danese to do something that she did not want to do.

I went in, and when they saw me, they ceased their conversation. We said good morning and had our breakfast. When we had finished, John told me he would be looking forward to my return, again with that delectable smile. Then he was off for a busy day. I wondered why Danese was not dressed for work and asked her if she was feeling all right. "Oh yes," she replied. "I have some personal business to attend to the next two days, so I am taking some time off."

When I finished my coffee, I went upstairs to call a cab, having returned my rental car the day before. I got all my things together and went down to wait. The car arrived, and I think we took the scenic route into town on the way to the airport to take my forty-five-minute flight from Virginia to Kentucky.

Mom was waiting for me when I got off the plane, and I knew what she was going to say before she said it, so I beat her to it. "I suppose we are going into the country, aren't we?" I asked.

"Yes, of course. Aren't you back a little early?" she asked.

"Yes, as a matter of fact, I am. I have a few problems to work out with Andy before I return to Virginia."

Kentucky was an alluring place. The mountains were impressive as we passed ranch-style houses and a few horse farms. I remembered how much I missed home. We drove for a while before reaching Mom's home. For some reason, I was looking at the house as though I had never seen it before. We turned through the black wrought-iron gate to go up the winding drive. As we reached the house, for the very first time I thought what an awe-inspiring house it was, brick with its four huge columns across the front of the wonderful wraparound porch. The rocking chairs were made from solid oak. I had never thought of our house as grand, but that was exactly how I saw it that day. The double doors with tall wreaths displayed on either side gave a welcome and inviting entrance. This might not be so impressive from the Kentucky point of view, but from mine, it invoked a real sense of pride.

I asked Jack, Mom's and my handyman, to bring in my luggage, and then gave him a gift I had chosen for him. Mom and I went into the living room, and I gave her the things I had purchased for her.

"Angie, dear, you do spoil me, you know."

"Oh, Mom, I love buying for others. This time, I must admit it was spur-of-the-moment."

"Never mind that," she said. "These are marvelous." I had given her a blown glass swan and an original Hummel piece for her collection. We had coffee and relaxed on the sofa. I must have been more tired than I realized, for I nodded off. When I awoke, I smelled an amazing aroma coming from the kitchen. Florence, our cook, always outdid herself when I came home.

"Smells like Italian to me," I said as I came into the kitchen with Florence's gift in hand. You would have thought an army was eating instead of just the four of us. I thought about calling Andy but decided not to, as he had probably already eaten or made other plans.

When dinner was over, Mom and I went into the great room and sat for a while in front of the stone fireplace. I often went to Mom and talked about everything. "Mom," I said, "I have a big problem with my story. The family I am writing about may have more history than anyone knows about. What would you advise? Should I explore the past or leave it be?"

"Angie," she said, "I can't tell you that, but you know what I have always said. If it will hurt anyone, why bother?"

"That's the problem. I don't know if it will or not."

"Well," said Mom, "find out first. If you find the problem to not be harmful, then you could reveal it."

"Yes, Mom, that's it. I should find out the facts first. You know, Mom, I know these things, but it always helps to talk with you. I just need to hear it from you. I miss our talks, and lately, I've been missing Dad."

"I know, dear, we will always miss your dad. I miss you and will be glad when you can come home."

Mom and I rarely talked about Dad. He was killed in a car accident when I was a teenager. Mom was very strong, but at times, I could sense how much she missed him. I often wondered why Mom had never remarried. She was not that old and was very attractive. I suppose it is true that there is one man who can make you completely happy. Maybe someday I would find out.

The next morning, I called Andy and asked him to meet me for breakfast. When I arrived at the restaurant, Andy was waiting, which was very surprising; normally, he was late. I showed him what I had, and he thought it was very good. He didn't even suggest any major changes. I did tell him that there was something I would investigate when I got back, that I felt like there might be a story in this one.

"Anything I need to know about, Angie?"

"No, no, it's just routine stuff. I want to work this out for myself. If I need you, I'll call," I replied.

"All right," he said. "But remember, don't go it alone if you need help." I agreed that I would not. At times, Andy could get very excited, even hyper, so I thought it best to explore on my own when I returned to Virginia.

I had been feeling very tired lately, so I made an appointment with my doctor, since it was time for my physical anyway. I wanted to know why I was so fatigued all the time. He did blood work and when it came back, it showed that I had markers for Lyme disease. I had been having flu-like symptoms, had some susceptibility to light, and they found a small rash on my stomach.

He prescribed a few weeks of antibiotics, after which I needed to find some green drinks to boost my immune system. I started the green drinks and found a healthy little restaurant to go to when I ate out but decided I would not go out as much. I spent the rest of my time relaxing and clearing my head so I could be objective when I got back. Mom and I spent the last two days of our time together going to the theatre and doing things neither of us enjoyed doing alone.

The next day, I would have to get ready to leave. It seemed as though the time had slipped away so rapidly. After my ride on Ginger, my favorite horse who had been my pal since she was a colt, I took her into the barn to brush her down, and I put her blankets on her back. I noticed Purrcy, Tobee, and Selma, our barn cats, playfully running around. When I got back into the house, I checked myself carefully for ticks.

The morning came all too soon. I got dressed and gathered my things together. Mom insisted on driving me to the airport. I promised to call her upon my arrival in Virginia. I had purposefully not called ahead. When the plane landed, I rented a car and drove out to the Tuckering estate.

I was becoming familiar with the drive now, and it really wasn't half bad. When I got to the estate, I went to the door and rang the bell, expecting Heidi to answer. Instead, it was Danese. She was a little surprised to see me. I apologized for not calling, but she told me not to give it another thought.

I dined with her and John that evening. John said he had talked with Andy about the rough draft, and so far, he was very pleased. I told him I would try to wrap up all the loose ends before the Christmas holidays and be out of their way.

CHAPTER 8

Following the Willows

I spent most of my days now rehashing and doing background work. My writing was coming along well. I had noticed a change for the last couple of days to John's schedule. I wondered what it could be. He was leaving after dinner. It could be a lady friend, or Mrs. Greenbrier could be telling the truth. I had to check it out of curiosity if nothing else.

After dinner, I went straight to my room put on my jacket. I took out my work and went into the library. I knew I would be able to tell when John left. Sure enough, he went out the door at 7:00 p.m. I went out after him. He got into his car, and I waited until he was off the estate. I got into my car to follow. Unfortunately, I was not a very good detective. I did not even know which way to turn.

I struck out. I would have to devise a plan for following him. Oh well. I decided not to waste a trip. I went on into town and took a long walk on the greenway. I was feeling a lot better even though I had not quite finished the antibiotics; I had so much more energy. I was glad I had taken the time to go because Lyme disease can become quite serious. Since it is caused by a tick bite, I had undoubtedly gotten it while riding Ginger. Lyme disease could even cause death if not caught on time.

The next morning, I was up early. I took a walk. I noticed Danese and her dog in the convertible again. She took the dog somewhere about once or twice a week. Maybe she was taking him for a walk on the greenway. I noticed that this was a Tuesday. I would watch her pattern and try following her the next week.

I went back to my room and was having my morning coffee when a knock came at my door

It was Johnese. This was quite unexpected. She wanted to know if we could do something together, maybe some shopping the next week. "Sure, Johnese." I wondered why she would want to go shopping with me, or anyone, after looking at clothes all day. We planned a trip for the following Monday. I knew it would be interesting.

That afternoon, I left before John came home. I went to a small, rather quaint café that served sprouts, green drinks, and other healthy foods. I grabbed some bean sprouts and a green drink and browsed in the bookstore nearby. At about 6:00 p.m., I drove back to the estate. As I approached the gate, I saw Danese was pulling out. She had not seen me, so this was a perfect time for me to follow her. We drove for about forty-five minutes. I followed her to a place called the Forrester Institute of Psychiatric Care. I turned around and went back to the estate.

My work was cut out for me. I would have to find out about the institute, who the administrator was, and a way to get in the door.

That evening, Heidi came to my room. "Angie, are you comfortable? Do you need anything?"

"No, thank you, Heidi, I am fine."

"I found this on the floor this morning." Heidi showed me a locket; a beautiful locket. "Miss Danese wears it all the time. I could never understand why Miss Danese had two pictures of herself in it. That Miss Danese is a strange one."

"I will be sure Miss Danese gets it back, Heidi."

"All right, Miss Angie, thanks."

I knew that Danese spent a lot of time in her room, but one of her favorite reading places was a little window seat on the second floor, so I decided to put the locket there so she would find it. Sure enough, she did. That night, I checked, and it was gone. In the morning, Danese had it on at breakfast.

Well, I had to do some research the next day, so that night I chose to look at the scrapbook Danese had given me and go back over what I had written on my book.

The next day came swiftly and passed that way as well. I found out the institute was supposed to be one of the best in the state. The administrator was Chuck Forrester. Now my only problem was how to get in.

I went over my choices that night. I thought I could simply confront John tell him I knew about the institute. I could speak to Danese. This was not likely. Danese was so frail in spirit; I doubted she could handle it at all. Well, I would take a day or two and get everything together and decide when the time came.

CHAPTER 9

Finding Janese

I decided to make an appointment with Mrs. Greenbrier. I needed to talk to her. I wanted her to know that, for some reason, I believed her. Maybe she could help me a bit. I really didn't know why, but I needed to talk to her.

Mrs. Greenbrier was a gracious lady. She told me to come by on Tuesday. I came by about 12:30. She answered the door herself she said her maid was off that day and thought it would be a good time to visit.

She asked me if I had done any research. I told her I had and that I had found evidence of another child. "I'm trying to find out more about her. Mrs. Greenbrier, is there anything else you can tell me about John Senior's wife?"

"His wife was Lydia Janese Morgan. He met her on a buying trip. She was from Chicago. When she left John and the children, she went back home. To my knowledge, she never saw the children again. She died about five years ago. I know this because Mrs. Satterfield, a neighbor of ours, kept up with her after she left. Mrs. Satterfield was her only friend. That is the reason I know she died. That is all I know about Lydia Morgan other than the twins look just like her."

Now that I had found out where Janese was I had to devise a plan. How could I get into this place?

I slept on my problem. The next morning, I opted to simply go to there and ask Mr. Forrester, if he chose to see me. I would explain that I was writing a biography on the Tuckerings. Maybe he would help me. The most he could do was throw me out.

THE CRYING WILLOWS

I dressed, went downstairs, and had coffee and a muffin I had bought at the health food store. Heidi was her usual self, still trying to feed me.

After breakfast, I went for a walk and sat on the bench I loved for a few minutes to think. Then I was on my way to try and talk to Mr. Forrester.

On my way, I kept trying to find excuses to turn the car around. I told myself I should be writing this morning. When I could not find an excuse to turn the car around, I just kept driving. Somehow, I was impelled to find out about this girl. I never liked to tell just a part of the story.

CHAPTER 10

Meeting Mr. Forrester

I pulled into the parking lot of the clinic. I sat there for a minute or so. I was very nervous. I knew I had to complete the task at hand. I said a little prayer and then went inside.

I walked into the lobby and thought how clean and how pleasant the place seemed. I went to the information desk and asked if I could speak to the administrator. She asked if I had an appointment, and I told her I didn't but I needed to talk to Mr. Forrester concerning one of his patients. She took my name and asked me to have a seat. She disappeared through the double doors behind her desk.

When she returned, she told me Mr. Forrester was in a meeting at present but if I could wait fifteen minutes or so, he would see me. I sat down and started going through some of my notes, making some more while I waited.

About that time I heard a voice saying, "Miss Larrimore." I looked up; it was Mr. Forrester, or so his name tag said. He was tall and had graying hair with a wonderful smile.

"I'm sorry, Mr. Forrester, I was caught up in my work. Thank you for taking the time to see me."

I followed him to his office, and we sat down to talk. It was a huge office, very traditional with the big mahogany desk. He asked me to sit down. I thought the chair in front of his desk was very comfortable.

I told him I was there to talk to him about Janese Tuckering. He looked shocked and asked, "How do you know the Tuckerings?"

"I need to explain to you that I am writing a biography on the Tuckering family. I found out about Janese and wondered if you would talk to me about her. I wouldn't have to talk to her, just you. I just need to know about her. John does not know I am here."

"I know you cannot talk to me without his permission." He said he really could not unless I got permission from John or Danese. "If you do get permission, though, I would be glad to allow you to see her. Someone needs to tell her story."

CHAPTER 11

Asking Permission

I went back to the estate and took a walk in the garden. I sat on the bench a while, thinking about how to go about telling them I knew about Janese. When I saw Danese's car coming up the drive, I went inside. I went up to my room to get my thoughts together. I had told Heidi I would be having dinner there that night. I could get a feel for the mood of everyone at dinner, then I would ask Danese if we could meet the next day.

At dinner that evening, we had a scrumptious meal. During dinner, Johnese was going on about a new design. Her dad was actually listening to her. Danese did not say much during the conversation.

After dinner, John asked me if I would like to go into the sitting room with the family. When we were seated, Heidi brought us all a cup of tea and left the pot. The fireplace was ablaze; it was just getting cold enough for a fire. I loved it; it reminded me of home.

John asked me how my work was coming. I told him it was going well. That gave me an opening to ask Danese if we could have some time together the next day so I could get some more information. She agreed to meet with me in the afternoon.

John and Johnese seemed to be getting along better together these days. John was getting a little more comfortable with me, and Johnese was always fun to be around.

I met Danese at her office. She and I were engrossed in a nice conversation. I then changed the subject and asked her if I could talk with her regarding her sister, Janese. She did not know quite what to say. Finally she asked how I knew about Janese. "I am a writer," I said, "and I am doing a biography on this family, so naturally I looked into your background. I would like to include all of the family and tell the true story."

"I cannot tell you anything about Janese unless John agrees. I will speak to him tonight alone after supper. We will let you know."

Now I thought I had done it. I went to the mall and walked around for a while. I took in one or two shops and bought a scarf for Mom. I concluded that when I got my answer from the Tuckerings, I would go back home for a day or two. I was glad I was so close to home on this one. I went back to the estate and spent the evening in my room watching net flicks.

The next morning, a knock came at my door rather early. To my surprise, it was John He wanted me to come to his office that day. They would talk to me. He asked that I be there at 3:00 p.m. I said I would. I figured I was going to write a great book, or I was going home for good.

It was finally time to find out my destiny. I got into my car and drove to their office; I tried not to think any negative thoughts as I drove. I went to John's office when I arrived. Danese was already in the room. John came in shortly thereafter, closing the door behind him. When we were seated, John got right to it. I thought I detected a little anger in his voice.

"I don't know how you found out about our Janese," he started, "but I want to make it clear I will not allow anyone to upset her or to make it look as though we just threw her away. That is not the truth. Janese was not like us. She was slow, and we kept her out of the limelight so that people would not make fun of her or treat her badly. We love Janese. She always thought as a child and still does. I will allow you to talk to her if she is all right with it. When you write about her, I want it to be the correct story. If you need information in the future, please come to me."

"I will come to you from now on when Janese is concerned. Thank you, John and Danese, for allowing me to see her. You do not have to worry. I will not write anything except the truth. I will tell your story the way you want it as long as it is the truth."

"All right, my dear, it seems as though we are on the same page."

"I will go tomorrow, if that is all right with you. I will meet Janese and talk to her with Mr. Forrester present, if Janese is comfortable with that."

CHAPTER 12

Bringing Janese Out

I called Mr. Forrester the next morning, and he said the best time for Janese was in the afternoon, about 1:00 or 2:00. So I made an appointment to meet her along with Mr. Forrester that afternoon at 1:00.

After pulling into the parking lot at the center, I sat for a moment, taking a deep breath and asking the Lord to help me with this endeavor.

Mr. Forrester was in the lobby when I entered. He asked me to sit with him in his office so we could talk a moment before seeing Janese. In his office, he explained to me that Janese would be as a child in her mind and that her moods could change at any time so we must be careful. Mr. Forrester and I entered the room. Janese was sitting on her bed playing with her dolls. Mr. Forrester said, "Hello, Janese."

Janese said, "Hi." Then her eyes went immediately to me. "Who are you?"

"My name is Angie."

"Are you going to be my friend?" she asked.

"Why, yes, I will be your friend." I sat down next to her, and she began to talk to me. She told me her dolls' names, and I played dolls with her for a bit. Then I said, "I like being your friend. Do you think I could visit you again?"

"Yes, I would like that."

"What else do you like to do?"

"I like to draw."

"Maybe we can draw when I come back. I have to go now, but I will come back to see you again."

Mr. Forrester was amazed. He said he had never seen her take to a stranger that way. He asked if I would come for a couple of weeks; I agreed to.

On my way home, I drove with my windows open; the breeze was warm but crisp. There was a crispness in the air. The breeze was beginning to blow; the trees were beginning to change their color.

As I travelled, my thoughts turned to Janese. What a sweet spirit. I just could not see why anyone would think this child incorrigible. We will see as time goes on. I felt a sense of accomplishment and hoped my relationship would make a difference in Janese's life.

I arrived back at the estate at dinner time. After dinner, I asked John if I could talk to him. He asked me to meet him in a half hour in the study. I went to the study at the agreed time. John was not there yet. Heidi asked if I needed anything. "No, thanks, I will just wait." I sat there reflecting on that dear, sweet child.

John came into the study and sat down. "I take it you have seen Janese."

"Yes, sir, I have. She has a very sweet spirit."

"You must have caught her on a good day. I'm glad that was your first impression. Don't forget it. I suppose Chuck told you that her moods were subject to change."

"Yes, he did. I will be seeing her twice a week. Mr. Forrester asked me to. We just played dolls and got acquainted."

"She must have liked you."

"Yes, Mr. Forrester was amazed at how she reacted to me."

"I have something for her. Would you like to take it to her?"

"I sure would, Mr. Tuckering."

"Please call me John."

"All right, if you will call me Angie."

"It's a deal. I'll be right back with the gift." He brought back a drawing pad and some watercolors.

"I will take them and tell her they are from you."

"No, just let her think they are from you."

"Well, if you insist."

It was getting a little late, about 8:30. I told John I would need to go write a little while, and we said goodnight. It was now about

9:00. When I got to my room, I resolved that before I started to write I would go out to my favorite spot on the balcony. I sat there enjoying the nice breeze. Then I heard them, the crying willows. I listened as they moaned their cry, and for me it brought comfort. I made the choice to tear myself away and go in and write. I wrote well past midnight before turning in for the night.

The morning brought to me an abrupt start. The phone was ringing. It was my mom. "Hi, Mom, how are you?"

"I'm fine. I just wanted to hear your voice. I miss you."

"I miss you too, Mom. Are you sure you are all right?"

"I'm fine. When do you think you can come home?"

"Well, about a month, but just for a visit. This book has turned out to be more than I bargained for."

"All right, Angie, I will call you later. I love you."

"I love you too, Mom."

That seemed strange. Mom sounded different. I would try to get home soon.

I needed to get up anyway. I got up, put on the coffee, and took my pill for my immunity. I had been taking it to rebuild my immune system ever since I had Lyme disease. As soon as I finished these meds, I should be back to normal. I grabbed a cup of coffee and headed to the balcony. I thought about Mom and how she would be so busy with her projects. The month would go by faster for her than me.

I sat contemplating what my day would hold. The willows were quiet that morning; there was a definite chill in the air now. I thought I might need a sweater before leaving the house.

I decided to visit Janese. I was very excited to see her again. Before going to the clinic, I dropped by my favorite bookstore and browsed a while, then on to the clinic. I was looking forward to my visit with Janese.

When I got to the door, Chuck Forrester met me and informed me today might not be a good day to visit but he would leave it up to me. "If you don't mind, I will go with you. I'm warning you, though, you are not going to see the same child."

When we entered the room, Janese was sitting in her rocking chair. "Hello, Janese," Mr. Forrester said. She did not say anything;

she just pointed to me. I saw that today was not going to be a successful one. I sat with her a while and walked out with Mr. Forrester.

"What changed in one day?" I inquired.

"I don't know. No one has been able to pinpoint what brings this on. Most of the time she is very sweet, sometimes very quiet and pensive as today, then sometimes she can be frustrated and even mean."

"Is there any warning when she changes?"

"No, not really. You should come back tomorrow. She could be totally different."

"Then I will see you tomorrow, Mr. Forrester."

"Please call me Chuck."

"All right, then."

When I went into the clinic the next day, Janese was her sweet self again. "Hi, Angie," Janese said.

"You do remember your friend."

"Yes," she said.

"I'm glad you do. I have something for you, a present."

She started clapping her hands. "Yes, a present!"

I gave her the paper and watercolors, and she said, "John sent them."

"Yes, John sent them."

"I like John."

"He likes you too."

I stayed a while and watched as she put her things into a chest. We played for a while, and then I said goodbye.

I was amazed that this was the same child as the day before. I went to Chuck's office and told him I appreciated his allowing me to see Janese but I felt I had learned all I could from her. He asked me to keep coming for at least another week. I agreed.

Back at the house that evening, I talked with John and told him I would probably only be going to see Janese for another week or so. I would stay at the house so I could get my writing underway.

I went straight to my room had an urge to go to the balcony. I sat there hoping to hear the crying willows. They did not make their sound that evening. However, the little frogs down on the pond were certainly chattering. I felt at peace out there. I reluctantly went inside and began to write. I had a very productive evening.

The next morning, I got up early and had an invigorating walk, envisioning I could be riding Ginger. I then saw Danese. I waited to pet Sadie. Danese had stopped to feed her birds. I talked with her a few minutes. The phone was ringing when I returned to my room. I answered the phone; it was Chuck He asked if I could come to the clinic that day. "Sure. Is there a particular reason?"

"Yes. Janese asked for you by name." Chuck was excited that Janese had asked for me by name. He said she had never asked for anyone by name except John or Danese. She had not actually asked for them but would say their names when they were there. "Thank you for coming. This could be a big breakthrough for Janese."

I went on in to see Janese after lunch. She was sitting in her rocker. She came over to me and stroked my hair and said, "Pretty Angie." Apparently, she liked raven black hair; a lot of her dolls had black hair.

I said, "You are pretty too, Janese." I talked with her for a while. We played dolls and fixed each other's hair. Janese was very talkative; she had a lot to say. I felt like there was a lot more to her than any of us knew. As I came out of the room, Chuck was coming up the hall.

"Angie, you really don't understand how much you have helped Janese. I have never seen her like anyone this much. I hope it won't inconvenience you to come for a while."

"Sure, I don't mind. I will come as long as I am here. That will be a month or two longer."

"Thank you, Angie, you don't know what this means."

That evening I talked with John. Although Chuck had called him about Janese, I told him I would be staying at least a month or two. He was also appreciative that I would be visiting Janese.

CHAPTER 13

Shopping with Johnese

I was sitting in my room when someone knocked at my door. I got up and opened it. It was Johnese. She asked if I wanted to go shopping, I said sure, though I didn't know why she was asking me. But I was glad; I loved shopping with her. We made a date for the next day. She said she was taking a trip and needed some things.

After Johnese left my room, I went on to the balcony for a final cup of coffee for the evening. Then I heard the willows crying soft and low, just enough sound to hear. It always comforted me.

I got up early the next morning, picking out some jeans since the weather now had a definite chill in the air. I layered up. I met Johnese downstairs in the library, and we were on our way. It was going to be a day of fun. I knew this because anything anyone did with Johnese was always fun.

We started at the mall, shopped there for about an hour, then had a bite of lunch at Johnese's favorite sandwich shop. After that, she took me to a couple of specialty shops in town. I found a necklace for my mom's upcoming birthday. We shopped for another hour. Johnese then wanted to get a pizza. The thought had not crossed my mind: she was almost young enough to be my daughter, so eating was something she could do nonstop. At any rate, we went to a pizzeria. I just had a salad and water.

We sat and talked for a while. I asked her if her trip was for business or pleasure. "I am hopefully going to make some money for the company," she said. "I am going to show my newest designs to a company in Paris, France. Maybe they will like them." She reflected.

"Oh, Johnese, they will love them. Who could not love your designs?"

When we were finished, Johnese asked if I wanted to watch a movie. I said sure.

I did not expect the kind of movie we went to. It was great. We went to a park that had a big screen set up on which they showed old movies. I could not believe that Johnese would appreciate the classics as I did. I inquired as to why she chose this theater. She said her dad used to bring her here all the time when she was growing up. "We still get away occasionally to see our old movies." So there was another side to John, a side I had not seen before that was refreshing to know. I was glad he was not as stuffy a businessman as he appeared.

After the movie, we went home. I told Johnese what a great time I had, and she was glad she had enjoyed the day as well. Johnese reminded me of a child. She was full of life and energy. I knew, though, her dad was the reason. She was such a great designer and was able to meet all the demands on her because of her dad.

I got to my room and thought about the outdoor theater. That did it for me; it was perfect. I hoped Johnese's trip would be safe and productive. I knew I had to spend the next two days in residence working on my manuscript. Andy would be expecting more of my work in a month or so. I had to get to work. I chose to turn in that night without listening to the willows.

The morning brought a fantastic array of color from the balcony. As I sat there with my morning pick-me-up, I listened as the willows cried a low but restful sound. I went to the library and worked the entire morning away. About 1:00 p.m., Heidi showed up with a tray of my favorite munchies. I thanked her and sat it down on the desk so I could snack while I worked. Before I knew it, I had an empty tray. I went on working. I was still working when I heard John and Danese coming in. I picked up my things, took the tray back to the kitchen, thanked Heidi, and told her I would be down for dinner.

I went to my room, took a quick bath, and put on nice attire for dinner. When I got to the dining room, John was already there. He pulled out my chair for me. I sat down, then Danese arrived. John also seated her We had a wonderful dinner, after which Danese went on upstairs, saying something about spreadsheets. I had not noticed before how amazingly handsome John was. He was tall with a great physique, and he had the most gorgeous black hair and the most wonderful blue eyes ever. We had a very pleasant conversation. I was a little surprised I had not seen this side of John before. I would like to see more of it.

"John, thank you for the great conversation. I've enjoyed it."

"I have as well, Angie."

"I will have to say good night as I have a little more work to complete this evening."

I started working as soon as I got to my room and worked until about 10:00 p.m. I concluded I had worked enough for one day. I put my things away and went to my favorite spot. The willows were crying loudly in the wind tonight. I heard a hoot owl in the distance. I thought it was all close to being perfect.

When morning came, I went to the clinic to see Janese. I went straight to her room. As soon as she saw me, she smiled and said, "Angie." We talked for a while, and she asked if I would like to brush her hair. Her hair was like Danese's; it was thick and copper in color. It was a stunning color. Even though they were fifty-two years old, neither of them had much gray in their hair. Janese and I had a lot of fun together. She combed my hair, and we combed the dolls' hair. Then Janese handed me her sketchbook and said, "See my book." There was no more paper. I promised to bring back some more. I wondered if Johnese knew about Janese. I left there thinking about Johnese, how she needed to know Janese, and how Janese needed to know her.

I drove up to the estate. Each time I did, I had to hesitate before I drove in; it was so beautiful. I drove around to the back side of the house where I parked and went in. When I reached my room, the phone rang. It was John. He asked me out to dinner that evening. I was shocked but reluctantly said yes.

As soon as I hung up, I realized I had to find something to wear. I tried on everything in my closet and finally settled on a little black dress with a black-and-silver shawl and black-and-silver heels. We were going to a little bistro he knew.

I put on heels because John was so tall; I needed a little height. I took my shower, dressed, then had to decide what to do with my hair. I usually wore it up or pulled back; tonight I decided to wear it down. I brushed my hair and let it fall down my back on the outside of my shawl. I waited in my room, putting on the finishing touches until John called my phone. I said I would be right down.

John always looked good, but you could tell he had tried to look good tonight. When I was downstairs, John told me I looked beautiful. "Thank you, John." We left in the Lincoln and drove to the bistro. It was a wonderful little place. It was quiet, elegant, and had a great atmosphere. We enjoyed dinner and had an interesting conversation. I was a little surprised that John and I hit it off so well. I was glad that we had. I decided not to ask if Johnese knew about Janese—not just yet.

As we drove home that evening, I saw John in a new light, one I thought I would like to explore.

CHAPTER 14

My Break

I called my mom the next morning. I told her to expect me the next day. She was elated at the news. I went by to let John know I would be leaving for about a week. "Have a great trip, Angie," he said.

"I will, John. See you about next Tuesday."

I chose to go see Janese. I did not know if she would realize what I meant. We were playing with her favorite dolls when I told her I was going to go home for a few days and that I would be back to see her. She stopped playing. She took my face between her hands and asked if I promised I would come back.

"Yes, I will come back in seven days." We marked the days on her calendar. I told her I would mark nine days in case I had to do something when I got back but I would be back by that time to see her.

I went back to the estate packed and called for my flight time. That evening after dinner, John asked me if he might drive me to the airport in the morning. I gladly accepted. I retired to my room and went to the balcony just before bed and sat quietly listening to the crying willows. That was one thing I knew I would miss.

The next morning, I had all my luggage carried downstairs. "Ready to go?" John asked. John and I took my luggage to the car, and we were off to the airport. We chatted on the way. When we pulled up and got my luggage checked, John said, "When you are coming back, please let me know. I will pick you up."

"All right, John, thank you."

"Happy flying."

When my plane landed, I got off and went to claim my luggage, and shockingly enough it was all there. Another surprise was Andy.

He drove me to Mom's house in the country. When we arrived, I saw that Mom had put out her fall decorations. Her yard was always pristine.

As I went in the door, I called, "I'm home!" Mom was in the kitchen. Jack had already gotten my luggage and was on the way in with it. Mom gave me a hug as I came into the kitchen. I told her I would put my things in my room and be back to help when I got back down. She was putting everything on the table. I helped to put the food on, noticing that everything she had fixed was my favorite. That was my mom.

"How long can you stay this time?"

"Only for a week. I'll probably be home for good in a couple of months. The book is going well."

"That is good news. I miss you."

"I miss you too, Mom. I'm glad to be home for a few days. I needed a break. I must see Andy tomorrow so we can go over the material. Hopefully he will not want me to change much. Then you and I can visit the rest of the time."

The morning came too soon for me. I called Andy and arranged to meet him at the library in town. To my delight, Andy was already there when I arrived. We sat down and hashed through the chapters I had already written. He had some small things changed that really didn't matter to me, so we had a great first session. When we finished, I told Andy that I had to complete this book in a couple of months. He was right; he had nailed it this time. This was the perfect family to write about. I had thoroughly enjoyed it

That evening, I drove home thinking I was glad this part of the trip was over. I told Mom to be ready to do anything she wanted to the next day. We said goodnight. I went to sleep very quickly; just being in my own bed was bliss.

In the morning, I was up at 9:00. Florence had made breakfast. Mom had asked her to serve us in the garden in one of our favorite spots. We had a pergola in the garden with a table, and that was where we had breakfast. She asked if we could just stay home that day.

"Sure, Mom. Are you feeling all right?"

"Oh yes. I just thought we could catch up a bit."

"All right, Mom, that's fine with me."

We spent the morning in the great room, my favorite room. The weather was now getting cool but not quite cold enough for a fire in the fireplace. I would be glad when it would be. Mom and I had a great morning together.

Mom informed me we might be having company for dinner. I didn't know whether I liked the sound of that. "Which of your friends has a single whatever this time?"

"No, no, it's a surprise. I hope you won't mind. He said he needed to talk to you. Oh, I might as well tell you, it's Luke. He said if you don't want to talk to him, he left a number."

"I'll be taking that number, Mom. That is the last thing I need."

"I know. I told him that is how you would feel. I will run and call him. And as for you, get dressed. We are going out tonight."

I took the number. I was nervous. He had a way of making me cave. I was unusually strong when he answered. I just said, "Luke, thank you for the invitation, but that won't be happening. Please don't call me or my mom again." Then I hung up. How could he after the way he treated me? We had been engaged. I thought we would be married; however, the day before our wedding, he left me a message on the phone—on the phone, mind you—saying he could not go through with it. Why did he even think I would give him another chance?

"Mom, are you ready?"

"Yes, let's go. We are going to have a good time."

"Anything you want to do."

Mom wanted to go to the antique shops. We went to most of the shops in town. We mostly looked but did find a thing or two, then we wrapped up the day by going to Mom's favorite place to eat. We had a family restaurant in town; it had been there most of my life. It had always been our favorite place to go. The food was always great; the atmosphere clean and homey; the people who ran it had been there many years and knew everyone. It made you feel as though you were going to an old friend's house.

Mom and I got back to the house about 8:00. I was ready to go write, and Mom was very tired. She went to bed, and I went to my room to write. The next morning, I contemplated taking a horseback ride. I went out to the stable and talked to Ginger. I decided it was a good morning for a ride. I asked Jack if he would saddle Ginger for me, and he did. I took a nice long ride and thought how much I missed this. When I got back to the stable and started to rub down Ginger, Jack took over. I went into the house. Florence had just finished up breakfast. I did eat that morning but asked Mom and Florence not to fix the morning meal for me as it just was not my favorite time to eat. They reluctantly agreed.

"What is on our agenda today, Mom?"

"Your Aunt Cindy wants us to come by today."

"Sure, Mom, I would love to see Aunt Cindy."

Mom and I drove over to Cindy's house. We had a fantastic time; we strayed the entire day. My Aunt Cindy was an eccentric character. She was my dad's sister. She was an architect and very successful. She had decided to retire the year before and travel. She had traveled to almost every continent in the world. She had always been my favorite aunt. We watched movies of all her travels. She always traveled alone; I really don't think I would have the courage to travel abroad alone. Nothing bothered Aunt Cindy.

Mom and I stopped for a pizza on the way home. We had a little ritual when we had pizza; we always had it in the great room, used our little tables to eat on, and played games all afternoon—checkers, cards, sometimes Monopoly. That night, we decided to play checkers, and a hand or two of Phase 10. We got carried away as usual and played games until midnight. Realizing what time it was, we both went to bed and slept in until 9:30 the next morning.

Mom wanted to just stay at home and rest; she seemed to need it after our day yesterday. My mom was very active but lately I could tell she was a bit tired, so I didn't argue about staying in. Mom was very active in the community; she and Florence had some meal planning to do! They were planning a dinner to raise money for the children's home, which they did twice a year. I thought it would be a good time for me to catch up on my reading.

Tomorrow would be my last day at home. I wanted to do something special for Mom that I knew she would like. I thought and thought; finally, I remembered how much my mom loved a picnic. I asked Florence to pack a picnic lunch for Mom and me the next day.

The next morning, I went to Mom's room about 10:00. I told her I had a surprise for her. I asked her to dress warmly and meet me downstairs in twenty minutes. She agreed. I had Florence put the picnic basket and a blanket in the trunk of my car. We got into the car and were on our way. When we turned into the park, Mom said, "Yes, a picnic! I'm glad you thought of this. I do love a picnic."

"I know, Mom."

She and I found a lovely spot overlooking the lake. When we were finished eating, we elected to take a hike. The three-mile trail was a rather short walk for us but that was what Mom chose for the day. When we returned to our spot, we sat on the benches at the lakeside and talked for about two hours. Unfortunately, our day had to end. We drove home, and I got packed and ready to leave the next day.

The next morning, Mom was up and ready to take me to the airport. I asked again if she was feeling all right. She assured me she was fine. We said goodbye. I was looking forward to getting back and finishing my task. I would miss my mom. I had thought about the estate, about Janese, and about Johnese's trip while I was away.

CHAPTER 15

The Estate Awaits

I landed at the airport. I had called John as he requested, and he came and picked me up. When he arrived and had gotten my luggage, I asked him if we could go by the clinic on the way to the estate. He did as I asked. When Janese saw me, she ran to me and gave me a big hug. "I have something for you," I said.

"You do?"

"Yes, I do." I had brought her another tablet to draw on and some barrettes for her hair. It made her very happy. John did not go to her room with me. I wondered why. When I came out of her room, I saw him talking to Chuck. I assumed he wanted an update on Janese. After our short visit, we went to the estate. I thanked John for picking me up and told him I would retire for the evening so I could relax and hear the willows cry.

"You like the willows too?"

"Yes."

"So do I."

I sat on the balcony listening to the willows cry in the wind, then I wrote for a while before bed. The morning brought another near-flawless day. There was no one in the house; Heidi was off for the day. I was almost glad I had the house to myself. I could go into the library in quiet solitude. It was a very restful and productive day.

I had decided it was time for me to ask John if Johnese knew about Janese. I would wait for the right time, though; I did not want to get on John's bad side.

I stopped working around 4:00 in the afternoon. I cleaned up my things and took them upstairs. I had a place to work in my room, but I liked working in the library.

Just as I got my things put away, the phone rang. I answered it; it was John. He ask me to dinner. I told him I would meet him this time; he said that would be great. He was going to visit Janese so he asked that I meet him at the Italian restaurant in town about six thirty. I said I would. I was relieved that I would not have to drive to Richmond this evening.

I met John. We had a lovely dinner. He informed me Johnese had called and would be coming home the next day. He would like to do something special for her the day after she returned and wanted to know if I could suggest anything. "I know the perfect thing," I said. "The outdoor theater."

"How did you know about that?"

"Johnese took me there once when we went shopping, and from the things she told me, that was one of her fondest childhood memories—she and her dad going to the outdoor theater."

"Thank you, Angie."

"You are quite welcome, John. Johnese is a lovely girl."

"Yes, she is. Would you like to join us, Angie?"

"No, not this time. This time should be just you and her."

I had settled back into my regular routine. I was writing a lot but kept thinking there was something else I must know. I just kept writing and searching. John had really never told me much about his father's accident; I only learned from Mrs. Greenbrier that Janese had shot him by accident twenty years ago. Someday I would ask for more details, if there were any.

I went to my room that evening thinking what a magnificent time I had spent with John. I must stop thinking of this place as being permanent; when the book was finished, I would be going back to my small but wonderful life.

The morning brought a little rain; it also brought to this house a hustle and bustle as if it were almost Christmas. Everyone was looking forward to Johnese's return. She was such an easy person to love—thoughtful, friendly, and a lot like her dad.

John was off to the airport at least a half-hour early. Heidi had been in the kitchen all morning. Danese had even been helping; I had never seen that before.

I went to the library to do some work. I felt this celebration should be a family affair, so I went out before Johnese got home. I knew she would want me to join them but felt this was just not the proper time; there would be other occasions.

I left and went downtown and found a little diner with great atmosphere. I truly enjoyed dinner. I called my mom to say hi before leaving the restaurant, then headed for the movie theater and took in a comedy. For some reason, tonight I just felt the need for laughter and to lighten my mood.

I drove slowly back to the estate. I saw two deer crossing the road on the way. The rain had subsided now, and it was now quite chilly. I thought about all the things I had learned about this one family and wondered how many more stories there could be. For now this was the only one I was interested in. I was ready to get through, but it looked as though I would be a little longer than I had originally thought.

CHAPTER 16

Andy

I was thinking of Andy one day. Andy and I had been friends through school. We had graduated high school together. He had always been one of my favorite friends. Andy was successful in everything he undertook. He was a great agent. He had a wonderful wife and two children—a little boy, six; and a little girl, three. I often went to dinner at their house. I was almost envious but was also truly happy for them. At times, I was still glad I was not married. Of course, there were other times I felt a little lonely.

Andy was always at the top of his class. I was smart, but Andy was much smarter. He took everything seriously but was not a stuffed shirt. When it came to work, he did not play around. That was why I wanted him to be my agent. He did a great job for me. He and I had had our little tiffs about this and that but we never had a real argument. As I said, he is one of my favorite friends. He had met his wife, Mandy, in college. They had a lot in common and seemed to have a perfect marriage.

Andy took my book for now, but I knew I had to get on with this story to please him so he would not be calling me all the time wanting to know what I had found out. Andy knew when to push me. He always knew when there was more to the story. That was why I was glad he was my agent. Sometimes I was a procrastinator.

CHAPTER 17

Mrs. Greenbrier

My thoughts turned to Mrs. Greenbrier. I wondered what else she could tell me about Janese. She must have gleaned more about the situation, having been their neighbor and babysitter all these years. I sat listening as the wind gusted through the willows; they seemed to clear my head.

The morning brought a delightful start, even though there was a nip in the air. It was still warm enough, though, and the trees were ablaze with color. The sun was coming up; it was a glorious start to the day.

I had gotten up early this morning so I could have coffee with Johnese since I had not had a chance to talk with her since she had returned from her trip. She was in the dining room having coffee as usual, so I joined her. "How was your trip?" I asked.

"It was wonderful—exciting and productive. You were right. They loved my designs. I did well."

"I'm glad you did. As I said, your designs are the best."

"You are up early this morning," she observed.

"Yes, I have a lot to do today. The book is coming along well. There are just a few more things I need to know."

"Can I help you?"

"I don't think so. I want to know about the first Mr. and Mrs. Tuckering."

"Sorry I can't help you there, but if I can, let me know."

"I will, thank you. Well, I'm off to work."

"See you later, Angie."

"All right, have a great day."

When Johnese had left the house, I went back upstairs. I did not want to see John this morning. I went to my room and found a notepad and put it into my purse. When everyone had left the house, I phoned Mrs. Greenbrier and asked if she would meet with me. She agreed and asked that I come to her house after lunch. I elected to walk to her house. It was such a beautiful day. As I walked along the sidewalk, I crunched the leaves as I did as a child. The tree-lined streets were eye-catching. The trees were now getting very colorful; the reds, the golds, the rust, and crimson. It was just my time of year. It stirs something within me to see all the beauty the Lord affords us.

I reached Mrs. Greenbrier's house and rang the bell. She opened the door herself. We went into a different sitting room at the back of the house. It was a lovely room. She had beautiful furniture, a bit different in style, more eclectic but beautiful.

When we were seated, I said, "Mrs. Greenbrier, can you tell me anything else about Janese's mother or about what happened when John was killed?"

"Well, let me see what I remember. When John's wife Lydia lived there, she always seemed to be very nervous. She was very beautiful and had alluring auburn red hair and green eyes, but she was always on edge.

"When she just had the twins, she would get me to sit for them when they would go out. Janese was always slow. She didn't walk until she was two years old, and her speech was not good until she was about four. She was not happy at times.

"Danese hardly ever cried. Janese cried all the time. I think that was one of the things Lydia could not take. When Janese was about three, she did not cry as much but she would get into moods where she would fight her mother. When Lydia got pregnant again, she was not happy. She did not want another child. John was so excited when he found out it was going to be a boy, but Lydia did not want another child. With the two girls and Janese being the way she was, I think was all Lydia could handle. She stayed until John Junior was two years old. The girls were five. No one has seen her since.

"The only thing I know is that John had enough money then to fight for the children, and I think Lydia thought she would not have a chance, so she left and went back to live with her family. She did not ask for visitation rights. Lydia did not have many friends. She was quiet and introverted, like Danese. She had one lady who lived in the neighborhood that was a friend to her. Her name is Patsy. She lives in the large stucco house with the red door. She might be able to tell you more."

"Thank you, Mrs. Greenbrier, you have been a lot of help."

That evening, I worked in my room well past supper, not noticing the time. I went down and grabbed some leftovers and took them to my room when I was a little hungry.

I began to think about the things Mrs. Greenbrier had told me. I thought about the woman named Patsy. She was the only one I did not have a last name for. However, I did have an address. I may just look her up. I would think about it awhile before I decided.

Mrs. Greenbrier was an old lady, but she had all her facilities about her. She knew about the people and she lived in the neighborhood when John Senior had built the first house. Patsy must also be an older lady, about sixty-eight maybe. Mrs. Greenbrier seemed like a good person, not wanting to gossip. I think she wanted to know about Janese and how she was. I was glad to have met Mrs. Greenbrier. She was a pleasant lady.

Chapter 18

Mom's Birthday

My mom's birthday was the next week, and I wanted to do something special for her. I could not go home again right then, so I didn't know what to do. I would have to think about it.

I went into Richmond one day because I wanted to see Janese before going to the clinic. I decided to go to the quaint little bookstore that I had visited several times before. I bought Mom a book and one for me as well.

I was going to have to come up with more than a book. I had spent most of the morning at the bookstore. This was not a strenuous task for me. I needed to grab a bite before I visited with Janese. I stopped at my new little healthy restaurant, and who should I run into but Johnese.

We had lunch together. She asked me what I was doing that day, and I told her I was trying to think of something to do for Mom's birthday but I wasn't getting anywhere and I wouldn't be able to visit. "Bring her here," Johnese said.

"Well, that's a thought."

"She could stay at the estate, and you could let me design her a dress."

"I couldn't impose on you all like that."

"It would not be an imposition. It would be me creating, doing something I love to do."

"Thank you, Johnese, for the generous invitation. I'll see you tonight. I must get on with my errands."

As I went through the door at the clinic, Chuck met me. "Angie, I don't know about seeing Janese. She is very agitated. She has not been happy all day."

"Could I just try and talk with her?"

"All right, but I will go with you."

"Sure, that's fine."

We reached the door. I could hear her yelling. We entered, and when Janese saw us, she stopped yelling. She went to her rocking chair and began rocking back and forth. I stayed across the room from her and talked to her. "Janese, it's Angie, your friend. I came to see you."

She stopped rocking, looked at me, and smiled. I still did not know exactly what to do; I just kept talking to her. She got up from her chair, came over to me, and asked me to brush her hair. So I brushed her hair and talked to her. She calmed down and went back to being that sweet child I knew. I wondered if anyone would ever figure out Janese. I stayed with her for a while, then told her I had to leave but would be back.

"Will you be back?"

"Yes, I promise."

She smiled at me. She picked up a doll and went back to her rocking chair.

I left the clinic thinking someday maybe someone can help Janese. I went into some shops along the way to get some inspiration for a gift. Nothing helped. Johnese's idea was sounding more enticing all the time.

I did hate to impose but I would pay her, of course. Well, I would think about it for a while. I did have a day or two to decide.

I decided to have dinner at the estate that night. That was one thing I liked about the Tuckerings—they always had dinner together. I suppose I needed a little normalcy in my life this evening.

We had a wonderful beef Wellington. Heidi was such a great cook. Maybe I should hang around her more when she was cooking, I thought. We had great conversation, and when we were finished, we went into the sitting room for a while. It was especially nice that night; the fireplace was ablaze. I loved the fireplace; it reminded me of home. It had finally gotten cool enough for a fire. I started to go to my room, and Johnese said, "Wait, Angie, I have something to show you." She had already started sketching my mom's dress or dresses. "Do you like them?"

"Of course, they're beautiful, but I really don't want to take advantage of you like this."

John spoke up and said, "Angie, think nothing of it. We would love to meet your mother. She would be welcome here." I reluctantly agreed but told Johnese the condition was that I pay her for the dresses. So we agreed.

I got up to my room and just did not want to work that night, so I gave myself the evening off, thinking all the while what Andy would say. He would always tell me an idle mind was wasted thought. Although I knew he was right, I just needed a little break. I wrapped up and went to the balcony. I told myself this was all right because I always got inspiration here.

The willows were making lots of noise that night. It was almost getting too cool to sit on the balcony. I would just have to dress warmer. As long as I was here, I would listen to the willows. I finally made myself close the door and get into bed. I would call Mom in the morning and see if she would even entertain the idea of coming over.

The morning brought beautiful sunshine, and although there was a definite chill in the air, I thought what a splendid day it was. I knew also that a sweater would be on my list that day. I would really need to get to work. I went to the kitchen and grabbed some coffee, then went straight to the library, where I would spend most of my day. About 2:00 in the afternoon, I realized I had not called Mom. I put away my things and called her.

She was unusually cheerful. I was glad I said hi. "Mom, I have a surprise for you, if you will agree."

"What is it?"

I told her I would like her to come to the Tuckerings' for her birthday since I could not come home just yet. She gave me all kinds of excuses. I knew the list by heart: she didn't want to travel alone; she could not be away more than a day or two. Finally, I told her it was not a long flight and I would pick her up at the airport. I would send her a ticket for the day before her birthday. She could go back home the day after. She finally agreed. I knew I had a lot to do.

First of all, I called Johnese to let her know. I would send Mom's ticket. She would be here on Tuesday and stay until Thursday evening; her birthday was on Wednesday. That made Johnese happy.

I sent Mom her plane ticket. Mom arrived the next Tuesday. I was there to pick her up. She was very happy to see me, and I her. When we arrived, Heidi showed Mom to her room on the second floor next to mine. She was as amazed as I was to see the estate. To be staying there, she thought, was her birthday gift. I told her I had a little more in store.

The next day, we walked out to the garden to sit on the bench and look at the superb garden which I knew Mom would appreciate. We sat and talked until we began to get a little chilly. We went into the great room to warm by the fire, then went upstairs. Mom came to my room for a cup of tea before we wrapped up and sat on the balcony for a while. I so wanted Mom to hear the crying willows. Once again, nature provided her symphony. We listened for a while. We finished tea, and Mom said she was going to turn in. I told her we had a big day the next day. She should be ready to go by 9:30 in the morning. That was fine with her.

The next morning, Mom came to my room. She was ready, and I was putting on the finishing touches. We left the estate. Mom didn't know where we were going. We pulled into the parking lot of the Tuckering Corp. building and went to Johnese's office. Mom hit it off with Johnese just as I did. She took Mom to her design room and showed her two dresses she had designed just for her. Mom was so surprised she did not know what to say. I had finally done it. Surprising my Mom was almost impossible.

She loved both dresses. Mom was very happy. I told Johnese how much I appreciated what she had done. I paid her and told her I would make it up to her someday. I ask if she wanted to go to lunch with us, but she had to decline because she had a meeting. Mom and I went to lunch at a little place I had found in the city, a little sit-down diner. I knew Mom would love it. Then we went to a quaint little bookstore that Mom liked as much as I. We browsed for a while, then called it a day. We went back to the estate and sat on the balcony, took one more walk in the garden before it cooled off, had another cup of tea on the balcony, and said good night. Mom thanked me for the day.

Mom and I had breakfast the next morning with John, Danese, and Johnese, and thanked them for this wonderful gift they had given to both of us. We could not have been together otherwise.

We had great conversation at breakfast. John was so gracious. He told Mom to come anytime she wanted. Danese was a caretaker at heart; she waited on Mom from the time she came in that morning.

Mom and I spent the day taking in nature. We went to the garden and saw two deer playing down near the willows, then we walked out to the kennel and petted Sadie, Danese's dog. We lingered outside awhile, sitting on the bench taking in the morning sun. Mom and I went inside, and she grabbed some tea, and me another cup of coffee, and headed for my balcony. We listened to the willows crying in the breeze and spent our day talking and catching up.

I asked Mom again if she was feeling all right. She assured me she was, but something was different. She did not seem to have as much energy. I knew as we get older, we don't have much energy, but I just felt something was wrong. I dismissed it as old age.

We had dinner with the family before I drove Mom to the airport. When we finished dinner, John offered to drive us, but I told him I would go; I had something I needed to do anyway. "But thank you, John." My mom said goodbye, and we were off to the airport. She promised to call me when she got back to the country house. That was a change. It was usually me promising to call.

CHAPTER 19

Talking to John

Again I found myself in a somewhat familiar spot. I wanted to talk to John. I needed to ask him if Johnese knew about Janese. I didn't think she did, but I had to find out from John. When dinner was over, I told John I wished to talk to him. We went into the sitting room. I said, "John, you are not going to like my question."

"Well, as I recall, I didn't like the last one, but look how that turned out."

"All right, here goes. Does Johnese know about Janese?"

"I suppose you have guessed the answer. No, she does not know. I should have told her long ago. The time just never seemed right. She does need to know, I just don't know how to tell her. I will work on it, though."

"If you need help, let me know."

"Thanks, Angie. I must do this myself."

The next morning, John came into the library where I was working. He informed me he had to take a trip. When he came home, he would tell Johnese about Janese.

John was going to be away, and Johnese and Danese would both be very busy in his absence. I was looking forward to John's return. I somehow knew Johnese would be better off for knowing and so would Janese.

I had a very good week. I ran into Danese while visiting Janese one day. She had Sadie with her. Everyone loved the dog, especially Janese and her friend Patsy. Danese was just leaving, so Janese introduced me to Patsy and told her she had to go to her room to visit with me but would see Patsy later. There was a Tuckering in there somewhere, and one day I believed we would meet her.

Janese and I went to her room and played for a while. We brushed hair. I left and told Janese I would be back on Thursday. When I went back to see Janese that Thursday, I took her some paper and colored pencils. She put them into her chest. I asked her if she wanted to draw with me. "No," she said, "I draw by myself."

"May I see your drawings?"

"No, I don't show them to anyone."

So we played dolls. I stayed with her a little longer that day. She asked me if I liked her friend Patsy.

"Why, yes, I do."

"Me too, and I like you too, Angie."

"I like you too, Janese. We can have many friends. It's good to have friends."

When I left, I wanted to take a walk, so I went to the greenway and took a very long walk. Then I stopped at some great antique shops and browsed for the rest of the afternoon. When I got home, I went to my room to write.

I would go back to see Janese the next day just because I wanted to. I worked until very late, then went to bed. My mind was full of thoughts. I was thinking about the estate and the people in it. All the people here were great people; they just needed to be put back together. I drifted off to sleep and slept until nine o'clock.

I chose to stay at the house and go see Janese the next day. I went to the balcony and sat for a while. The day was grand; the sun was warm. I didn't have to have my throw on as the sun would be warm until about five o'clock before it would start to cool. I went down to the library and worked for a while. I had Danese's scrapbook with me. I thought I needed to refresh my memory about what was in it.

As I was flipping through it, I stopped at an old photo. It was of John Senior and who I supposed to be Lydia, his wife. I thought she looked like Janese and Danese—the same hair and eyes and slender build. I had not noticed this picture the first time, so I kept flipping back and forth to be sure I had not skipped anything else.

I stopped writing for the day. Time had sort of slipped by without my noticing. I grabbed some fruit and went back upstairs, not intending to come back down. It was past 6:00 now. I knew it was too late to go see Janese, so I definitely would go tomorrow. I took a shower and got into my pajamas, wrapped in my throw, and went to the balcony. I sat there listening to the willows. They had decided to communicate tonight. It gave me a peaceful feeling. I stayed out until 9:00, then went into my room and wrote for a couple of hours before I went to bed.

The morning was a pleasant one. The breeze was coming in the window at the balcony. I had left the door cracked open so I could feel the freshness. It made me feel exhilarated. I got up and dressed. I skipped breakfast. I knew I was going into the city and figured I would need food at some point. I needed to start watching what I ate. Lately I had been eating way too much of the wrong things. I had still been exercising, though.

I took my time this morning getting dressed. It was still hard to know how to dress for the cool in the mornings and the evenings but the warmth in the middle of the day. I definitely needed an overshirt; I always started layering up as soon as the chill came into the air. I was finally off.

I stopped at the end of the drive and waited as the wild turkeys crossed, thinking how wonderful nature was and how it gave us small bits and pieces of wonder and excitement. I went on my way and stopped at the bookstore for a while. I found a wonderful poetry book that I actually bought, knowing I would not have much reading time until my own book was finished, but I would get around to it. I love poetry; it is so refreshing and different. Noticing the time, I paid for the book and went to the clinic to see Janese.

She was glad to see me. She was in a good mood today. She played dolls with me and gave me something in an envelope. I started to open it, but she said, "No, not until you leave." So I waited. We played awhile. When I had to leave, I thanked her for my present and told her I would be back soon.

I went to the car. I was curious as to what my gift was, so I opened it. She had pressed a flower between wax paper. A dried flower I supposed she had picked from the garden at the back of the clinic. How sweet and thoughtful she was. On my way, I did stop and eat but chose better today. Then I stopped on my way back to the estate to take a walk on the greenway.

When I got back home, I went straight to my room to work. About that time, Heidi came to my room with a cup of tea; somehow, she always knew when I needed it. She said my mom had called. I thanked her for the tea and the message.

I called my mom before I got into my work. She was fine; just wanted to talk. I told her I was doing fine and would be home in a couple of months. That seemed to please her. It actually made her happier than I thought it should. I suppose she did miss me, but she stayed busy with her community projects.

I started writing and forgot the time. When I realized it was 1:00 a.m., I went to bed.

John was returning that day. Heidi came up and asked me if I would join them. I told her I would. I knew I was also going to have a lot of balcony time. I was just going to relax today and hope to hear the willows. They obliged. They sounded wonderful. I had missed them as I had not had time for them in a few days. I must find something to wear. I didn't gab my jeans this evening; for some reason, I wanted to look good. I searched my closet and settled on a dark purple dress with a scooped neckline and a little sleeve that just came over the shoulders with a split from the shoulders on both sides. The dress was form-fitting with a little wispy scalloped tail just at the knees. I thought I looked all right. My black hair always looked better accented with diamonds and earrings.

I waited until 6:15 to go down. When I went into the dining room, John was already there. He got up and pulled out my chair. I thanked him and sat down. Johnese and Danese came in about that time. He, being the gentleman that he was, also seated them. Heidi than began to bring in the drinks. The food was on the table. She had outdone herself. I ate too much.

John asked if we could talk after dinner. I said sure. When we had finished, John suggested a walk in the garden. He said he was going to tell Johnese the next day. He was a little nervous about how she would take the news about Janese. The night was a little chilly. I must have looked cold. John took off his coat and put it around my shoulders. His touch made me tingle. I tried to put this out of my mind. I thanked him. He asked if I wanted to go inside. I said no, I would like to sit on the bench for a while. "I like the evening."

"So do I. It is my quiet time."

"Mine too."

We sat and talked awhile, then I said I suppose we must go in. "You probably have a lot to do," he said. "I will tell Johnese after dinner tomorrow evening."

"John, she will be fine. She may be angry with you, but she could never stay angry with you."

"I hope you are right."

"I'm sure of it."

"Well, I will see you tomorrow." He leaned over, put a little kiss on my cheek, and said thank you.

"For what?" I asked.

"For helping put this family back together."

I handed him his coat. "Oh, I suppose you will need this back. Thanks for the loan."

I must say I was a little enamored with John this evening.

I went to my room; John went to his. I didn't feel like working tonight. My head was full of thoughts of this place and all these people, especially John. I needed a little willow time, so that was what I did. I listened as the willows quietly whispered their beautiful sounds to me. I listened for a long time and just relaxed. That was just what I needed.

The morning brought a rainy day. I never liked rainy days. I was going to make myself go see Janese today, and then back at the estate I would work the rest of the day. Janese was in a bad mood when I got to her room. She appeared to be angry. I had just happened to bring some drawing paper. That seemed to make her happy. I decided I would always bring her drawing paper. She thanked me and put it away. Her mood changed. She got her dolls, and we played a while. I told her I had to go but said I would bring more paper when I came back.

"Good," she said. "I like paper." I wondered if she would ever tell me what she did with her paper.

That evening, I went straight up to my room and wrote through dinner. About an hour later, I heard Johnese. She had gone to her room and slammed the door. I took it that John had talked to her. I took a break and went downstairs, knowing there would be some leftovers. I got a hamburger bun, heated some pulled pork, and made a barbecue sandwich. When I took a walk in the garden, John was sitting on the bench. I said, "I'm sorry, I'll go."

"No, don't, please stay."

"I take it you told Johnese."

"Yes. She did not take it well at all."

"Well, she will come around."

"I hope you are right."

"You will see, she will. Well, I better get back upstairs. I do need to work this evening."

John took my hand and said, "If you are interested, we could run into one another in the garden tomorrow after dinner."

"Maybe we will." I went back to my room and got wrapped up in my work. I heard someone talking outside. I went to my balcony and saw that it was Danese talking to John. She seemed upset. Then they stopped talking and went inside. I sat on the balcony awhile listening for the willows to cry, and they did. It was as if they were talking just to me. I cleared my head and went to bed.

The next morning when I was going down to the library, I heard Johnese in the kitchen. When she realized I was there, she asked me to have coffee with her. I did, of course. She brought a carafe of coffee with her and two cups into the library. I saw that I was not going to get much work done. I said, "It is nice to see you, Johnese," for lack of anything else to say, but she, being her father's daughter, came right to the point.

"You know about my aunt Janese."

"Yes, Johnese, I do. I have been going to see her for a while now."

"What is she like?"

"She is a very sweet lady with the mind of a child. She plays with dolls, brushes my hair, loves art paper and colors but won't share her drawings with me."

"Would you take me to see her? I would ask my dad, but I am a little mad at him right now." I thought how much like daddy's little girl she sounded.

I told her I would. "But I want you to do me a favor."

"What is it?"

"Will you take some sketches and show them to Janese?"

"Sure, I'll get some. I'll get dressed and we will go." So off we went. In my mind, I was hoping this was not a mistake. You never knew how Janese would be with someone new.

We went to the clinic. I went in first; Johnese came in behind me. Janese said, "Angie," and rubbed my hair. Then she said, "Who?" pointing to Johnese. Johnese told her name and that she was John's daughter.

"I hear you like to draw," said Johnese.

"Yes, I do."

"I do too. Would you like to see?"

"Yes."

When Johnese showed her sketches to Janese, Janese began to clap her hands. She went to her trunk and pulled out book after book of sketches of her own. We were astonished at the sketches. They were sketches of doll clothes. "Janese, I think you and I will be best friends," said Johnese. Janese clapped her hands again. Then we all played dolls, and I told Janese we had to leave. She asked Johnese if she would come back.

"Of course," said Johnese. "Best friends have to visit."

When we got into the car, Johnese asked if we could go to the office. "I need to see my dad."

"Sure, Johnese. I'll wait for you."

She went inside, and I got out of the car. It was a beautiful day; I had to enjoy just a few minutes of it. I walked in the grass, kicking the leaves about, then sat down on the bench at the sidewalk and waited for Johnese while enjoying every moment of this glorious day. How the clouds were drifting in the sky, and the breeze was blowing a little cold through the trees. The leaves were now falling quite fast, and I knew winter was on its way.

CHAPTER 20

Johnese's Engagement

That evening, I had dinner with the Tuckerings. No one had to ask if Johnese was over her mad spell; it was evident.

She told her dad about Janese's drawings. "Danese, did you know about them?"

"No, I didn't. I do remember she was always drawing and was wonderful with color as a child. She had never shown her drawings to anyone, according to Chuck."

Johnese was so excited, like a child at Christmas. "When I go see her again, we can exchange drawings. That is what I want to do."

"Sure," said John. "Just don't get her overexcited. She has mood swings. She can be different at times, so be careful."

"I will, Dad, but she is a Tuckering."

"Point taken, my dear."

I excused myself just before dinner ended and went to write. I seriously had to, although I would rather be going to the garden. At least part of me wanted to go to the garden; the other part of me thought that it might not be such a good idea right now. I wrote until late in the evening. At the end of the week, I was getting ready to go to the clinic when my phone rang. It was Johnese. She wanted to go see Janese and wanted to know if I would meet her for lunch. I said sure, and she told me to meet her at the coffee shop.

I dressed and was on my way. I did not know what Johnese was up to but I knew there was something. Johnese had some sketches with her. We went into the clinic. When Janese saw us, she ran to Johnese and asked if she had pictures. "Yes, I do. Which one do you like?"

"This one."

"If I give you this one, may I have one of yours?"

Janese thought for a moment. She went to her trunk, got out four of her sketches, and asked Johnese which one. Johnese chose one. I still did not have a clue why but was sure I would find out. We stayed with Janese awhile, then left. Johnese wanted me to meet her at the clinic the next so she could see Janese. I agreed.

I went home and worked the whole day, then went to the library and closed the doors, hoping I could get a little quiet time. I worked for a while, then went up to my room.

I got up early the next morning, went out, and saw Danese getting ready to walk the dog. I asked if I could walk with her. "Sure," she said. We walked at a rather rapid pace. She was glad Janese and Johnese were getting along so well. "I didn't think it was a good idea," she admitted, "but turns out it was." I petted Sadie and told Danese it was good to walk with her. I went in and got ready to meet Johnese at the clinic.

Johnese had a box in her hand. I didn't ask. When we got into Janese's room, Johnese told her the box was for her. When she opened it, it was a little girl's dress made from one of her sketches. Janese clapped her hands. She went over and put it on her big doll. Then she went straight to her trunk, pulled out all of her sketches, and gave them to Johnese. "I suppose this is Janese's line," I remarked.

"That's right."

Then Janese gave her a sketch and said, "For me."

"You want this dress for you?"

"Yes."

"Okay, I will make it for you." Johnese started a new line of clothing for children and called it Aunt Jan's. Of course, somehow I knew it would be a hit.

CHAPTER 21

The Early Tuckerings

The day brought an urgency for me to finish my book all of a sudden; I knew I had to find the rest of the story. I went to the library and was glad I was alone in the house this morning so I could get some work done.

I went to the shelves and looked at the books at random. I saw a book on the top shelf called *The Early Tuckerings*. I got it down and found a lot of things. I found when John and Lydia were married and when their children were born. After John Junior's second birthday, though, there was nothing personal. There were things about the business. In the very back of the book, I found John Senior's death certificate. The death certificate said that John Senior was cleaning his gun when it went off and he was killed. I decided to ask John about the accident and see if he would talk to me now.

There was a little pouch in the back of the book with an envelope in it. I took it out ad looked inside. I found divorce papers for John and Lydia. I also found a letter from Lydia. It read,

> John:
>
> I can no longer be there. I cannot take care of three children. I told you I did not want children in the first place. I tried hard, but Janese is impossible for me. She might not be for others, but she is too much for me.

I am going home. I will not be coming back.
I will send divorce papers and custody papers. They will be signed.

I do love you, John. I do love the children. It is just not for me. You and I are opposites. You want all this, I just do not.

I wish you well.

Love always,
Lydia

I put the letter and the divorce papers back into the envelope and returned it to its pouch. I put the book back on the shelf. This explained a lot. This woman had married a man whom maybe she did love but she did not want children. When she had them, she could not cope, and she left. Not every woman wants children, though most do. I suppose that John Senior thought that when she had them, she would change her mind. But sadly she did not.

I went up to my room and made some notes to think things over. I would try to talk to John tonight; I did need to know if what the death certificate said was what happened to John Senior.

After dinner, I asked John if we could talk. He said yes. We went into his study. I said, "I have another question for you. Of course you are not going to like it. I wouldn't ask you if I did not need to know. I have just been putting it off. I want everything I write to be accurate."

"All right. I will tell you if I can."

"John, I need to know what really happened when your dad was killed. I knew you would have to know. I have just been putting it off."

After a moment, John said, "My dad loved guns. He hunted some. Janese was in the room. She saw the gun in the corner. She was always curious. She took the gun in her hand. I'm sure it scared Dad when he saw her with the gun. He went over to her. It scared her and she turned. The gun went off. She might have pulled the trigger by accident. It was an accident, so the sheriff and the coroner ruled it an accidental death and kept Janese's name out of it. We found Janese hunched in the corner of the room rocking back and forth with her hands over her ears. Danese and I did not know what to do, so we called our neighbor, Mrs. Greenbrier. She was the only one who knew about Janese, she and a few others. The sheriff and Patsy, his wife who lives down the street, the coroner—of course they were Mom's best friends. Dad would not take her places with us. He wanted to protect her from ridicule.

"When Mrs. Greenbrier agreed to watch Janese, we took her there and called the sheriff. He came out and took pictures, examined the gun, and, of course, found Janese's prints on it. The sheriff's wife Patsy had been my mom's best friend. He waited for the coroner to pronounce. We took Janese later to the cemetery and told her that Dad was sleeping with Jesus. That was the only way we knew to explain to her. She had not ever mentioned it or asked about him since, but she is still afraid of loud noises. Especially unexpected ones."

"Thank you, John. I know you do not like to think about it, but I do want to write it correctly."

I went to my room. Now that I knew the facts, I didn't know if I could write them. Is it so wrong to hide people's skeletons? I suppose most people have them. So I wrote in the book that John Senior was killed in an accident at home. Not exactly a lie but not exactly all the details. I thought Janese deserved that much. Another bit of history in the pages of time. I had just a few more things to wrap up and I would be leaving. I wanted to go home. I missed my mom. I was also beginning to form an attachment to these people and this house.

That evening, I was sitting on my balcony when the phone rang. It was John. He wanted to know if I would be his date for the evening. He had to take some prospective clients out to the theater. I said yes because I love the theater and had not been in a while. He said he would pick me up at seven. I started getting ready. I chose a pair of black dress pants, a black top with silver sequins, my black four-inch heels, and a small black handbag with silver trim.

I put my hair up this evening and wore a choker necklace with black and white diamonds and my black and diamond ring.

I went downstairs. John was not down yet, so I went into the library. I was just looking around when John said, "Angie, you look amazing."

"Thank you, John."

"Shall we?"

"Certainly."

I did so enjoy the theater. We had a great time. When we got to the estate, John leaned over to me in the car and said, "I had a wonderful time."

"So did I."

Then he kissed me. I did not respond because it took me by surprise, but I so wanted to. John then said good night, flashing that gleaming smile. I said good night and went to my room. I wanted to put the kiss out of my mind, but I had a hard time. I didn't want to go there; now was just not the time.

Now I had learned about the early Tuckerings, there was actually no story in the story; it was just as John had said, so that was what I would write, anyway.

CHAPTER 22

John's Wife

The next morning, I was up early. John was having coffee when I went into the kitchen. "Good morning, Angie," he said.

"Good morning, John."

"I had a great time at the theater."

"So did I."

That was the extent of that conversation. We had our coffee together, chatting about basic things, then it was off to the office for John and back to work for me.

In the scrapbook that Danese had given me, there were pictures of John Senior's wedding. It was a beautiful wedding. Cynthia, Johnson John's wife, was simply elegant. She had a gorgeous white dress with a long train. Her veil was edged with beads and gold sequins. The little sleeves that draped over her shoulders had the same sequins that also appeared at her tiny waist. Her shoes were gold slippers. Danese was the maid of honor. She was the only one I recognized in the wedding party. She was standing with a very handsome man; they seemed to go together. I looked on through the scrapbook and found where Johnese was born; pictures of the baby and of them bringing her home. John's wife, Cynthia, was very frail. She was skinny and had a weak look about her.

Well, another puzzle solved. If I kept piecing together things as I had the last couple of weeks, I would be done with my book soon. I thought I would spend a little longer in the library as it had proven so helpful to me these past days. I was browsing in the same section where I had found the early Tuckerings when I spotted a notebook, a black one with nothing on it. That automatically made me curious.

I took the book and went over to the desk and opened it. It was John's memories. I couldn't help myself. I read them. I felt as if I was prying. I just had to know what it said.

There was a chapter in each section. The first section was entitled "The Quiet One;" the second "My Beautiful Daughter;" the third one "My Special Sister;" the fourth, "Danese's Bond."

One more piece of the puzzle. An inspiring one. Something else I would have to get permission for.

That evening after dinner, we were sitting around the fire. I was glad; I loved this special time, with everyone together chatting about their day, their plans, the weather—anything, and just being together. In a while, it dwindled down to just me and John.

"I have another question for you."

"What would that be?"

"I found something today in your library. I hope you will be all right with it. I have not read it all, but I did open it and browse through the title of the chapters. It makes me curious, and I wondered if I could read it and use it in the book." I pulled out the black notebook.

"Oh my, I had forgotten all about that. Those are things I wrote about the family. I see no harm if you think you can use them. Just remember I am no writer."

"John, thank you so much for all you have done, for allowing me to stay here and being so cooperative. I appreciate everything. It looks as though I will be finishing my book in another month. Then I will be out of your hair."

"Angie, it has been a pleasure to have you. I think you are a delightful breath of fresh air. I hope you will not forget about us when you are finished."

"I don't think I could ever forget such a place and its people." I bade John good night and went to my room. I would read through the book and make some notes. One more thing I realized I would truly miss would be the crying willows.

CHAPTER 23

The Quiet One

The first chapter was about Danese. It read,

> I am writing this memory about my sister Danese. She is a very special sister. I love her because of her quiet nature and sweet spirit. Danese as a young person was always serious and very intelligent. She was very beautiful. Also she had a lot of boys ask her out, but there was only one for her. He was the best man at my wedding. His name was Dalton. He was an accountant. I was not surprised when they announced their engagement. It was to be a joyous occasion, and little Johnese was going to be the flower girl. Johnese was only three years old.
>
> One night, we were scurrying about, putting up the Christmas tree. Danese kept looking at her watch. Dalton was late. About that time, the doorbell rang. It was a highway patrolman. He had come to inform Danese that there had been an accident. Dalton was in critical condition at the hospital. Danese went right away. Dalton's parents were already there. They allowed Danese and his parents to stay in the room. Danese would not leave his side. Before his parents got back from getting coffee one morning, Dalton died.
>
> Danese was beside herself. When she finally calmed down, she called the house. I went and

got her. The next days were awful for her. She got through the funeral and the burial. I thought she would never pull out of that horrible depression. It was a month before she could even function. I finally talked her into coming to work for me on the business end because she is good with numbers. She did come to work. At first it was to pass the time, but in a few months, she did enjoy her work. She never dated again. I am sorry to say I wish she had. She is a very lonely person.

At times, I see the old Danese. I think she would like to be her again but just does not know how to get back there. The dog has helped, and her walks, and feeding the birds. Christmas is a particularly lonely time of year for her.

All in all, though, Danese is a good person. She is very strong when it comes to business deals. She can negotiate with the best of them and has a great business sense. She is great with figures. She and I have always worked well together.

She is settled and quiet, just a meek soul upon this earth, put here for me. When all the hustle and bustle gets too much for me, I can always feel the calm quietness about Danese. She is who I go to in those times. She always knows the things to say. She helps me to see things through her eyes, and they don't seem near as drastic.

When I think about the two of us, I think of my mom and dad. I am just like my dad, and what little I know of my mom, she is a little like her with the Tuckering gift.

I call her the quiet one because that is how I see her, as a quiet, meek soul that helps us all to calm down and enjoy life to its fullest.

CHAPTER 24

My Beautiful Daughter

The next chapter read as follows:

> My daughter, the most precious gift in my life. She is so beautiful, even though she looks like me. She has beautiful red hair, gorgeous green eyes, and a smile that could warm any room
>
> My daughter had always been privileged but has never thought of herself as that. That is why people love her, and that makes her beautiful. Her kindness and generosity is evident in her life. She likes to help those who are unfortunate. Her mother had died just after we bought Johnese home. I was really glad Cynthia got to see her at home in her nursery, which she had put together for her. I missed my wife so.
>
> Every day, from the time Johnese was little, she would draw. She loved to color. You might say she had always been my little designer. She went away to design school, and I knew she would be a good designer. What I did not expect was a great designer. She had exploded on the scene, so to speak. It was a fresh new era for our company.
>
> Johnese does not even realize, but she had her whole life ahead of her. Young people think so much differently than older ones. She thinks that the here and now will be her life forever. I

hope she is wrong. I know that someday she will want to marry that special someone and have her own family. That is the farthest thing from her mind now, but I am sure that is in the "someday" category of her mind.

As I read and began to write about these people, it gave me a new appreciation of each of them.

Danese overcoming her tragedy showed the strength of her character. Johnese so full of life; someday, no doubt, she would be the CEO of her father's company. She certainly had the ambition.

Heidi, as I read, came into the picture when Johnese was born. She came as a cook and nanny for Johnese. Heidi ended up being a cook after Johnese was grown. Johnese was such an enjoyable child; everyone pitched in and helped during that time.

Speaking of Johnese, I had to stop writing and meet her at the clinic. We were going to see Janese. Johnese had a big box with her. When we went into Janese's room, she did not respond to us. She was in her rocking chair. When she saw the big box, she said, "Is that mine?"

"Yes, it is. I brought you a present."

Then to our surprise, that same sweet child emerged. She opened the box like it was Christmas. When she saw the dress that she had drawn and that Johnese had made, she clapped her hands. She had to put the dress on that instant. It was a beautiful shade of purple. She loved it. Then we had to brush hair. I fixed hers, then she fixed mine. We looked into the mirror. She was pleased with herself, turning around and around, admiring herself. We had a great afternoon with her, then we left.

I went back to write for a while, then I went to the library. I browsed for a while and finally settled on a book. I wanted to read; it would be nice just to sit and read a book. I read until late on Saturday in my favorite spot, listening to the willows again. It dawned on me I would not be here much longer, and I would miss this place and these people.

CHAPTER 25

My Special Sister

The third chapter in John's book of memories had this to say:

> I have another sister. She is a twin to Danese. Her name is Janese. Janese is a wonderful person. She is slow, yet she is great at coloring and sketching things. I knew she had some talent; apparently, I did not know how much.

No one knew about our sister. My parents did not want Janese to be exposed to people who would ridicule her or treat her badly. We taught her at home. Danese was very good with her. She could always calm her down when she became agitated.

Janese went to a home to live when my mother left us. I guess it was too much for Dad. However, that home changed ownership, and Janese could no longer stay there. Danese and I begged Dad to allow us to bring her home, so we did. Danese took her over. She taught her things that no one thought she could learn. She taught her to write. She did not have to be taught to draw or anything about color; she already knew all that; it was already within her.

Her mood swings began to get worse. You never knew how she would be from one day to the next. When the accident happened, it set her back. We really could not keep her at home anymore. That is when she went to live at the Forrester Institute. It had been good for her. We have always gone to see her and brought her things.

Reading about Janese made me feel good and bad because of the accident. She will never forget that, but knowing what John said about her makes one know he really did love her and had her best interest at heart.

I suppose timing is everything now. Janese was introducing her new line of children's clothes called Aunt Jan's. It was a success. I have seen some of her mood changes, but I still prefer to remember this sweet-spirited little girl I first met.

CHAPTER 26

Danese's Bond to Janese

Danese did have a special bond to Janese; twins always have that. They can feel things about the other that no one else sees. Danese would invariably know when Janese was up at night. Danese would slip quietly to her and see what she needed.

Danese missed Janese when she had to go away. I remember when we were still young, my dad would take us to see Janese. We could take her presents. Danese always wanted to stay longer. We would play with our sister. We love her, we just didn't know what to do when our dad died. We were young and knew that no one knew about Janese. We had promised our dad we would always keep it that way. It had been very hard for us, but we have managed to do it thus far. We would have a lot of fun with our sister on our visiting days. Most of the time she is a sweet little girl.

My sisters Danese and Janese used to play in the garden. That was the only place we had to play. The garden seemed to calm Janese down when she became agitated. Even now she takes a walk in the garden. Every day she and her friend Patsy go there to talk. Danese takes Sadie the dog to see her in the garden. I think Janese remembers the good times in the garden at home.

When Danese was with her, she always seemed to be glad that her sister was there; it made her very happy. When we had Janese at home, she and Danese were together all the time. She helped her do everything.

Now Danese goes to see her a least once a week—sometimes twice if she can. She and Janese have always had a special bond that draws them together. When Danese was little, she t6old all her friends that she had a twin sister. Everyone just thought she was making up an imaginary friend. As she grew older, she understood not to mention Janese.

My thoughts about Danese is that I can understand why she is a caretaker. I saw her as a strong individual, a trooper, to have gone through everything she has and come out the person she is today, quiet and accomplished. We were now at the end of John's memories, which proved to be most helpful for my research. I would let John see what I had done and finish my book.

CHAPTER 27

Johnese's Designs

Janese, the twin considered slow, had more talent than anyone knew. She had books and books full of sketches of clothes, children's clothes. Johnese was certainly glad; it gave her an opportunity to do a new line. "Janese," she had asked her one day, "do you mind if I make a store for all the clothes you sketch?"

"Yes, I would like that." It seemed to make Janese very happy.

Johnese asked John if she could take Janese to the store when she got it opened. John said he would think about it. Johnese rented another space in the mall and was going to fix it up for a children's shop with all of Janese's designs. She always did things as if she knew it was going to work. I was proud of that determination; it always paid off. She worked on the shop in the evenings while her design team and she worked all day on the new line of designs. It was going to be time to open the shop before long. In another week, she put up the sign "Aunt Jan's." She felt a sense of pride when she looked at it.

John decided it would not be such a good idea to take Janese with all the hustle and bustle, and her being afraid of things as she was. Noise always bothered her.

Johnese decided she would take Janese after the mall had closed, so one evening, she explained to Janese she wanted to take her somewhere. She took her to the store. She showed Janese all of her designs hanging in the store. She was happy. She went to every piece of clothing and touched them. She looked all around the shop and clapped her hands and said, "Mine."

I said, "Yes. Thank you, Janese, this is a help to John."

"It is?"

"Yes, and to the whole company."

"I helped?"

"Yes, you helped," said Johnese. "You are a part of us, Janese." I took her back to the clinic a happy lady.

On my way home, I thought about Janese and about what she brought to our lives. She was such a sweet soul. She was certainly a Tuckering. "I never saw my grandmother," Johnese told me, "but each time I think about my dad, Danese, and especially Janese, I wondered what she was thinking giving up on such potential as we all had."

CHAPTER 28

My Rough Draft

I got my book together. I worked very hard over the next two days and finally got everything together. It was all ready and now I would make Andy very happy. I would call him in the morning and let him know that I would be sending my completed book.

That night I had a sense of peace. It always gave me a sense of relief when I finished a book. I would also call Mom in the morning and let her know I was finished, and as soon as I got my rough draft back and made sure everything was good with John, I would be coming home in about three weeks. That evening, I went out on the balcony and enjoyed my evening listening to the crying willows. I knew that I would miss this place and these people. I must stop thinking of them as part of my life; they really were not. They had been a chapter in my life. As I thought back over things, I thought sadly that most of my life had been this way from one book to another in my little fantasy worlds.

I went to bed and tried to put all my thoughts away and deal with things as they came.

The morning seemed to come very quick. When I woke up, I called Mom. She was very happy and excited that I would be coming home. I then called Andy; he was elated I was finished. He promised to get my rough draft back as soon as possible. That usually meant about three weeks. I hoped it would be that soon.

I would have some time on my hands. so maybe I could take in some theater and maybe even a shopping trip. As for today, though, it would be just a day of rest. I needed a break after so many hours of writing. A walk in the garden that morning proved very refreshing.

THE CRYING WILLOWS

The fall flowers were blooming; the leaves were turning their beautiful crimson and gold, rust red, yellow, and maroon. A wonderful beginning to a wonderful day. I watched as the squirrels stored their nuts in a nearby tree. The deer were drinking at the creek. A fleeting little red fox ran swiftly in front of the willows. A perfectly alluring day.

CHAPTER 29

My Book Publishing

It had been almost three weeks. I had taken in net flicks and read a few books. John and I had gone to the theater and to dinner a couple of times. Johnese and I had shopped for things for me and for Mom, of course.

I was really wanting to call Andy and see if he could tell me when my copy would be getting to me. I was getting anxious. I told myself to calm down. About that time, the phone rang. It was Andy. My copy was on its way.

I was so glad. I would talk to John. He could read it and make sure he approved of everything, then we could get together. My book would arrive on Wednesday, so I would read over it then ask John if he could meet with me on Friday. He could read the book and get back to me. Then we could move forward with the publishing.

When evening came, I told Heidi I would be having dinner with them. When dinner was over, I asked John if I could have a moment. We went into the study. I told him I had a rough draft of the book I would like him to see. He was happy.

"Would you have some time on Friday evening or Saturday to read over the book and see if it's all right?"

He agreed and asked me to dinner the next evening. I thought it could not hurt, so I agreed. I did like John and I thought there might be more there, but now was not the time to explore that. I needed to get through this book, go back to my little apartment, my mom, and my life, and see how I felt then.

When John called the next evening, he took me to a delightful little restaurant, one we had not been to before. He wanted to know if we might take a walk on the greenway afterward. I said I would love that. The dinner was fabulous and over too soon.

We walked on the greenway. John stopped, turned to me, and said, "I really don't want you to go, Angie. I feel we have something special."

"Oh, John, I feel we could have, but right now I have to go back to my life and see how I feel."

He kissed me, and this time I kissed back. We sat on the bench and talked for about an hour. He said he understood. Then we finished our walk and went back to the estate.

When John was through reading my book and thought it was all right, it would be time for me to schedule my departure.

Over the next few days, I was trying to enjoy the garden and, of course, the crying willows from my balcony. John finished the book and came to my room asking if he might talk to me. I went down to his study and he said everything was more than all right. I was grateful that he liked it. He went on to say, "I wish I could find something wrong with it so you would not have to leave. Speaking of which, when will you be leaving?"

"Probably next Tuesday."

John asked if I would have dinner with the family on Monday evening. I accepted his invitation. Before I departed, John took me in his arms and kissed me passionately.

I decided to go see Janese the next day, take her some paper and colors. I went at 1:00 p.m. to see her and stayed until three thirty. This was a longer time than I usually stayed. We played dolls and brushed hair. Then she did something she had not done before. She went to her trunk, pulled out a sketch, and gave it to me. I thanked her. I didn't know how to tell her I was leaving, so I just said I was going on a trip but would be sending her some things from time to time, which I would do. That seemed to satisfy her.

I told her I had to leave now. She gave me a big hug and stroked my hair. I left thinking that there was one great thing that came from this book. I had brought this family together somehow.

I sent my book to Andy on Monday. He got it right back to me to tell me we were going into publication. I was happy, but some part of me was a little sad. My book would actually be out in about six months. I dreaded the next few days. I'm not good at goodbye. My thoughts must turn to what lies ahead for me. I must leave the willows in the capable hands of this wonderful family.

CHAPTER 30

My Goodbye Party

Two weeks went by quickly. I went to see Janese on Monday since I knew this would be the very last chance to see her. We played dolls and I told her my trip would start tomorrow. She was in a fair mood today, but I could tell something was wrong. She did not respond at first, then she went to her trunk and pulled out a sketch with a big X on it. She shook her head and said no.

"Well, then, Janese, you will just have to try again."

She looked at me and said, "I did." She pulled out another sketch of the same dress; it also had a big X on it.

I smiled at her and said, "We all make big X's sometimes. We just have to keep trying."

Then she smiled at me and said, "Okay, I will."

I left that evening, thinking that Janese was not so much different from the rest of them after all. I intentionally stayed out until dinnertime. When I got into the house, I did not see anyone. In a minute, I heard Johnese calling to me. I went to the back of the house, and there they all were. The entire family and a huge dinner set up under the pergola and the firepit ablaze. I was shocked. I never expected this. I was speechless. I finally gathered my thoughts and said, "Thank you, all of you have been so wonderful to me. I could not have had a more pleasant stay anywhere. I will miss all of you."

We had a lovely dinner, and I almost dreaded to see the end. We sat by the firepit as long as we could until it was just too cold. I told everyone good night and went to my room. I had to pack the last of my things and run some last-minute checks to see if I had forgotten anything.

I would have to turn in my rental car that morning. John wanted to drive me to the airport. I agreed. I dropped off the car. My luggage was in John's car, so off we went to the airport. John went to the gate with me. I turned to say goodbye. John said, "I will miss you." Then he kissed me. I was glad I was getting on that plane so I would not have to think about the kiss or John for now. However, I did recall I enjoyed that kiss.

I was finally on my way home where my little apartment waited. My mom and Jack and our cook, Florence, back to my life in Virginia. I was on my way home.

CHAPTER 31

Missing the Willows

I got home and went to my apartment to unpack. I called Mom and told her I would be out to the country house the next day. I needed a little rest.

I unpacked went over my apartment, cleaning up the dust that had gathered, then I went right to bed. I lay there thinking how much I missed the crying willows. I got up and opened my window just a bit so I could feel the fresh air. It did comfort me somewhat. I still had a hard time falling asleep.

In the morning, I woke up and took my time getting dressed. I drove out to the country and enjoyed the drive. It was nice to be home again. I would have a little time with Mom and ride Ginger.

I settled in at home and thought I would stay until the end of the week. I so enjoyed talking with Mom and sharing everything I had been through the last few months. We talked about how beautiful the estate was and the peaceful sound of the willows.

I told her about Janese and how I had enjoyed her and needed to send her some things. She loved paper and colors.

It was nice to take a ride on Ginger that day; she was my favorite horse. I took a long ride. When I came back to the barn with her, Jack was there; he groomed her for me. Jack was the one who taught me how to groom her; he taught me everything I needed to know about horses over the years. Someday I would teach it to a child of mine. Jack had been with us for such a long time. We thought of him as family.

When I got back to the house, I asked Mom if she wanted to go shopping. She said, "Not today. I have an appointment." I did not ask what kind of an appointment. With Mom, you never knew. All of her community groups and committees were important to her. I just assumed it was something like that.

She went on her way. I still felt like a shopping trip. I went to our little mall in town. It would be Christmas before you knew it. Although it was just fall, and the leaves had just turned and began to fall, I knew it would fall fast and I needed to get ready. I would shop for Mom today since she was not with me.

Before I went home, I stopped at my favorite bookstore. Dina, the store owner, came to me and wanted to set up a book signing. I told her to call Andy and we would get it set. It made me feel good that she wanted to do one. I did, however, have to let Andy handle all of that; he was my agent.

I browsed in the library for a while and phoned Mom to see if she wanted to meet me for dinner at our favorite Greek restaurant; she said she would see me at 4:00. I met her and we had dinner. This was Florence's night off. We always carried Jack a plate back because he liked Greek food.

On our way home, our conversation was good. "How was your day, Mom?"

"Oh, I have had better."

"Is something wrong?"

"Oh no, dear. How was your day?"

"It was good. Dina asked me to have a book signing. I told her Andy would have to set it up, but I would be glad to do one as soon as my book is out."

"That is great, honey. I am so proud of you."

Mom retired to her room a little early when we got home. I assumed she was just tired. I really didn't think much about it as my mom had always liked her privacy. I told myself it was nothing.

Andy called the next morning and informed me we would have a book signing the next month as soon as the book was out at Dina's. I put the date into my calendar.

I asked Mom once again if she was all right; she of course said yes. I told her I would go back to my apartment. I wanted to get ready for my book signing and I also wanted to see if I could get another book started; not an autobiography, though. This time just a nice novel. This time, everything I wrote would just be in my head. I said goodbye to Mom and told her we would have lunch in a couple of days at our favorite sit-down diner. She agreed.

I headed to my apartment. It would be nice to have a few days. I needed to get my hair done, pick out some new clothes, that sort of stuff; clean my apartment thoroughly. Then I could carry on. Get my book signing over. Maybe I could determine how the book would do based on the number of people that came out. That was not always true, but sometimes it was.

I worked very hard these two weeks. I did all the little humdrum things. The apartment had to be the cleanest in the city; I was relentless with my cleaning this time.

The morning burst on the scene with another beautiful day. There were hints of gold, crimson, yellow, orange, and rust. My favorite season. The sun was glistening through the trees, making the leaves shimmer. How beautifully and wonderfully made. Sometimes we get a glimpse of how awesome heaven must be.

A little kitten showed up at my door. I would see if I could find its owner. I searched and searched. No one claimed it. I definitely could not keep it in my apartment. I would look for the next two weeks after the book signing. If no one had claimed it, I would take it to Mom's house, where it would fit in as a barn cat along with Selma, Purrcy, and Tobee, the barn cats we already had.

I made a Saturday appointment for my hair and nails. I had three days before the signing. I did all the things on my list. Tuesday was grocery day. It usually took me most of the day. I went to several stores to shop. I got fresh produce at a stand down the way, then I had to shop for shampoos, soaps, all those things. I did shop for some of these things on the Internet sometimes; I just felt the need to shop for some things in person. All my paper products, trash bags, storage bags, things of that nature I sometimes bought over the Internet. Today, I would definitely have to shop for cat food and a litter box.

I called on Saturday to see if I could get a massage. I figured I might as well make it a true day of pampering. I got my hair and nails done and had a massage and headed back to the apartment much more relaxed than when I had left.

In the afternoon, I worked a while, then called Mom. I told her I would see her at church on Sunday. We would have lunch at our favorite diner. Church was amazing that morning. I suppose I just had been ignoring that part of my life. I knew I needed to work on taking the time to be at church every Sunday. We all say we don't have time when actually time is all we have.

After church, Mom and I enjoyed our traditional Sunday lunch. Afterward, I went back to the country house and spent the afternoon. I checked on the kitten. Mom had decided to keep it in the house until it was a little older, then she would take it to the barn. She named it Tabitha; in case it was a boy, she would call him Timmy. I said goodbye to Mom and started my drive back into the city.

It was hard to believe it had been a month. Mom had said how proud of me she was and would not miss my book signing on Tuesday. Mom said she loved me before I left. That was a little unusual. She only said that when I was going away. I thought Mom was acting a little strange. After my book signing, I would investigate.

The book signing was a success with my mom, my Aunt Cindy, all my friends, and lots of people I did not know showing up. You never knew how a book would do. The major bookstores would tell the tale.

CHAPTER 32

Book Signing in Richmond

My phone rang early on Thursday morning. It was Andy. He had news. I had a book signing in Richmond and several more around the area. That meant I would be there for at least a week or more.

Oh well, so much for forgetting the willow's call. Andy booked us a hotel for the following Monday. Our first book signing was that Tuesday. I was right around the corner from the Tuckerings' company. I was almost dreading it, underneath all the excitement. I told Mom I would call her when I got to Richmond.

We left on Monday morning. When we arrived, we went directly to the hotel. I felt there was no need for me to rent a car as everything would be in walking distance. Anyway, Andy would be renting a car and staying in Richmond this time, the entire two weeks.

That meant he was going to do some promotions for the book. I would probably have to be photographed for a small article in the paper. I knew Andy. He was good at his job. Without him, I would not make near as much money; all this stuff was not my cup of tea. I had to go along.

We settled into our respective rooms. I worked a little on my new book. I had not told Andy about it yet. I would tell him when I knew I really had a story to write.

We had a day in between the book signing as it was not until Tuesday, so I thought I would go see Janese. I asked to borrow Andy's rented car on Wednesday; he said yes. I stopped on the way to get her some barrettes and a scrunchie for when she put it up.

I went to the clinic. When Janese saw me, she was happy. She clapped her hands. I gave her the gifts. She had to put some barrettes in right then. I stayed with her all afternoon. I had missed her so much. We had a great time, then I told her I had to go, I would be back soon. I would be here for a little while.

The lady at the bookstore wanted me to come back on Thursday and sign books again, so I agreed. The book signing started at ten o'clock in the morning and lasted until three o'clock in the afternoon. I was signing books when I heard a familiar voice, one you could not mistake, an energetic voice I had grown accustomed to. It was Johnese. She had come to get a book. We chatted a few minutes. I signed a book for her and one for John and said, "Tell him hello for me."

I signed books all day. I felt like I never wanted to write anything again. I was a little tired. Andy and I went around the corner to the coffee shop to grab a little bite. I had another day to go at this bookstore, three others in Richmond in the coming week, and one in Charlottesville. I knew my hands would be cramping by then.

Andy and I had just gotten seated when I saw John coming straight for the table. "Hello, Angie."

"Hello, John."

"Hello, John. Won't you join us?" Andy said. He sat down, and we talked during dinner, just small talk.

As we were finishing dinner, John said, "I would like the both of you to come and stay at the estate, if you will."

Before I could respond, Andy said, "Yes, John, thank you. That would be wonderful." Oh no. I could see Andy's brain turning in his head like a computer that could not be turned off.

I suggested to Andy after I said a few other things to him that we wait until after the book signing the next day to go to the estate. I called Heidi and told her what time we would be arriving.

Well, the willows surely called me back. I would be going back to the estate tomorrow. I would just have to deal with it. So much for forgetting. I would just get into my next book and take my mind off things.

CHAPTER 33

John's Invitation to Stay

John's invitation to stay at the estate had paid off. It was nice to be back in the room listening to the willows cry. I knew Andy had something up his sleeve.

It was book signing after book signing for the rest of the week and most of the next in Richmond. The last week, I had the book signing in Charlottesville, so it proved to be convenient. Before you knew it, I was shopping with Johnese for a new outfit and getting my hair done again. Andy, I knew, had something he wasn't telling me.

He had the newspaper team coming to the estate to do an article for the paper. I suggested we do it at the edge of the garden in front of the willow trees, which is what we did. I was glad I had gotten my hair done. The wind was not really blowing but there was a breeze. I admired the garden; it was lovely. The leaves all around gave an added glory to the shot.

We finally finished all the pictures, and they wanted to go inside to interview me. I took them into the library as I had done a lot of writing and research there. I was just not about to share the balcony with the world except in my book.

We did finally finish up all of the things I had to do. There it was: finally, time to go back home.

I started to pack. There was a knock at my door. I was a little surprised. I thought everyone was gone. Andy had gone to call and talk to Dina and check with the newspaper. He would be back in a couple of hours, then we would leave.

I opened my door. It was John. I did not know what to say. John started to talk first. He said, "Angie, please don't leave. Stay here a couple more weeks. Please give me a chance to know how I feel about you. I want to kiss you even as we speak. I think you feel the same way, you just won't let yourself. Please stay a couple of weeks. We can see where it leads."

"John, I will stay a couple of weeks. I want to see Janese again, and I do feel something for you. I suppose I could spare two weeks. I am not promising anything."

"All right, Angie, thank you for staying."

When Andy returned, I told him I was staying two more weeks. "Oh, really?"

"Oh, Andy, I have started a new book, and this will give me a chance to have some time by myself." I called Mom to let her know I would be staying two more weeks; not that everything was going fine. I had not yet packed, so I would not have to unpack. I did ask Andy to take me to rent a car on his way to the airport, and he did.

My decision to stay was a spur-of-the-moment thing. I did not know if it was a wise decision or not, but time would tell. I went to see Janese as soon as I got my rental car. I told her I would be there a while longer and would come to see her every week until I left. We played dolls and had fun. That evening, I was sitting on the balcony listening to the wind in the willows and thinking how pleasant this was and how much I had missed them. Thoughts of John came to mind. I knew I loved John, but I needed to have time to think.

CHAPTER 34

A Pleasant Stay

This stay did turn out to be a pleasant one. John and I began to see one another. There were many evenings at the theater. We watched net flicks and went skating. Once we went to the outdoor theater, which was one of my favorite things to do. There was something about sitting in the park with a picnic basket watching a large screen outside. We were having a good time. I was really enjoying being back at the estate, the shopping trips with Johnese, and visiting with Janese. It was as if I had a home away from home.

I had been there for a week already. It had passed very quickly. I had another week to go. I went to the bookstore and to the library. I attended a reading one evening. I was really enjoying myself but had really not thought much more about John except I knew I liked his company. I did have a wonderful time with him; I just needed a little more time to really know if we had anything we could build on. I thought so, but I needed to be sure.

I went to see Janese the next morning and took her some paper dolls. I had actually found paper dolls in a magazine and ordered them for her. I thought she might get a kick out of changing their clothes, and she did. It made her happy and me glad I had gotten them for her.

As I said, it was already Friday. I just had a week left; the time had flown by. I was dreading the next Friday. I went up to the balcony to do some thinking. My mom called while I was sitting out there. We talked awhile, and I enjoyed her conversation. I told her I would be coming home next Friday. That seemed to make her happy.

During the next week, John sent me flowers twice. He took me to dinner once, and we returned to the outdoor theater, my favorite thing to do. I went shopping again with Johnese to get a couple of things to wear. Johnese and I spent the afternoon together. She was always so much fun. I could see her dad in her.

I went home that evening. I had only two days to go. John said he wanted to take me out on Thursday night. He said it was a black-tie affair. Then he said it was just dinner, which meant it was a super nice restaurant. It would be a special dinner. That night I went up to my room and listened to the willows. I went ahead and packed my things.

Thursday was here. I wanted to look special. I went through a few things I had left out and chose a blue cocktail dress and my sapphire necklace. I thought I looked all right. When John looked at me, I knew I looked better than all right.

When we were on our way, he said, "You look sensational."

"Thank you, John. I just wanted to look special for a special dinner."

We went to a fantastic restaurant. We had a lovely dinner and a great time. Just before dinner was over, John took out a box. He took my hand and said, "Angie, I have something for you. You don't have to make any decisions right now. Just tell me you will take it and think about it." He took out the box and opened it. It was the most glorious ring I had ever imagined, and the largest one. It was a huge solitaire diamond ring with sapphires on either side.

"John, I don't know what to say. I am leaving tomorrow."

"I know just take it and think about it."

"John, I need to know what you are asking me."

"I am asking you to marry me. You do not have to answer right now. Take the ring. Keep it until you decide." He gave me a passionate kiss that made me tingle all over.

We went to the door. He pulled me close, once again wrapped his big arms around me, and gave me another passionate kiss. He made me feel so safe, as if nothing could ever hurt me again. He told me he loved me, and he hoped I would marry him. "I don't know," I said. "I do think I love you, but I just have to be sure."

The next morning, John drove me to the airport. I was boarding the plane. John pulled me close and kissed me and whispered in my ear, "I'll be waiting." My flight home was pleasant and not very long. I was glad to be back home. I was more confused than ever but back home.

CHAPTER 35

Some Thinking to Do

When I got home, I called Mom and told her I would be coming out tomorrow. I knew I needed some time to think things over. I thought going home, riding Ginger, checking on the new little cat Tabitha, and staying with Mom would bring me back to a sense of reality. I was afraid that the estate and all those people might be my fantasy world. I did not want to make a mistake.

John deserved better than that. He was a good man. He had waited a long time to open himself up to anyone. I wanted to be very careful and know for sure that I did love him enough to become his wife. The only way I would know that was to be away from him for a while and see how I felt. That was why I came home. I had not told Mom about the ring or John's marriage proposal. I wanted to wait for the right time.

I called John to let him know I was home. I could tell he was busy; he always took the time and was patient despite his busy schedule. When we were ready to hang up, he told me he loved me and said, "I'm still waiting."

"Goodbye, John, I'll be thinking of you."

I thought something was going on with Mom but could not pinpoint anything. I would just enjoy being home and spend more time with her, and whatever it was, she would tell me.

Over the next few weeks, I tried to keep busy. I talked to Andy about my new book, and we talked about the biography, which was doing quite well. All was well with my little life right now. Well, almost all. I still had not put the ring on yet; I would take it out, try it on, and imagine what it would be like to be able to live in that wonderful place and be able to listen to the willows all the time. Then I would take the ring off and put it away. I did miss John. I missed him a lot. I had called him once already. I had decided I would let him do the calling the next time.

Mom and I went out for the day. First, we took a long walk on the greenway. Then we did errands, which I hated doing: grocery shopping, things of that nature, things I was not used to doing because as long as I had some fruit yogurt, whole wheat snack crackers, and, of course, coffee, I was fine.

At Mom's house, we actually had to buy groceries, so I went with her and honestly tried to pay attention to what she bought. We all have certain things we like. I helped to pick out the groceries this time so that if I ever needed to, I could do this for her. I don't know when this would be. Mom was so independent. I think this was the first time I had ever been to the grocery store with her since I had moved to my apartment at eighteen years old.

That evening, we stopped and picked up a veggie pizza at Mom's request. We took it home and indulged in it. It was nice to be able to go into the great room after dinner and sit by the fire. We sat for a long time just talking about things we had not talked about in a long time: about my dad and about this house. Mom asked me if I would like this house if anything ever happened to her. I said sure.

She wanted to go the following week to see her lawyer and draw up the necessary papers, so I said all right. I asked her if anything was wrong. She said, "No, I just want some peace of mind to know that this will be yours. I'm not getting younger, you know. That is the way it works."

"I know."

"All right, we will do that next week."

I knew eventually I would have to tell Mom about the ring. I thought it would be before she gave me the house. I would ask Mom to have dinner with me at our favorite sit-down diner on Friday night, and I would tell her.

Over the next couple of days, I tried to put everything out of my mind to just enjoy riding Ginger and being with Mom. That was just what I did. That night, I received a phone call from John. I wanted to tell John I was going to tell Mom about the ring and the proposal but decided I better wait. I wanted to do one thing at a time: Mom first, then John. We talked about everything, about Johnese and Janese, Danese and the dog Sadie. When we were ready to hang up, John said, "I love you, Angie," and this time I said it back.

Friday had rolled around quickly. I needed to find the courage to tell my mom. I knew she would be happy for me, but somehow, I just had a picture in the back of my mind of Luke and what he had done. I know John was not at all like Luke. I tried to put all those negative thoughts out of my mind and be happy.

I dressed for dinner in some jeans and a long-sleeved shirt. I was glad tonight was a dress-down occasion. Just Mom and I at our favorite diner. It would be fun; we would be able to relax and talk awhile.

Mom and I left the house and drove to the diner. We got out favorite seat. This seat overlooked the pond at the back of the restaurant. We always liked to sit here, especially in winter, and watch the ice skaters as they gracefully skated on the pond.

We had our dinner. I could put it off no longer. "Mom, I have something to tell you."

"What is it, dear?"

"Well, I'll show you." I took the ring out of my purse.

Mom began to cry and said, "Oh, Angie. John is a wonderful man."

"I know. I have not said yes yet."

"Why not? Are you having second thoughts?"

"No, Mom, I just need to be certain."

"Your dad would be so proud of you."

"I know. Mom, I do still want the house, and I will always keep it."

"Well, young lady, I intend to keep it for a few more years, you know."

"Of course, Mom. I love you. I will see John sometime next month. I will then tell him I will marry him."

"Oh, honey, I am so happy for you."

"Thanks, Mom, I am happy too. The first time since all that stuff with Luke. I really thought I could trust no one again, and I suppose that is why it had taken me so long to say yes. Each time I think of getting married, I still think about what happened with Luke. I know John is not that kind of man and I know we will be happy forever."

CHAPTER 36

Finding Out Bad News

The morning brought more beautiful sunshine and gorgeous color, a perfect morning for a walk. I walked through the garden and on down to the stables. I just petted Ginger this morning. I was not up for a ride, but I did need some fresh air. My Lyme disease was gone but I still had days when I felt a little sluggish. I was still taking some vitamins and had finished the antibiotics; however, I was resting more normally and getting a lot of exercise.

Mom and I went out the next day. I noticed she was not her usual vibrant self. I asked if something was wrong; she said, "No, I'm just tired." I grabbed a Greek salad to go, and she and I went home and had dinner together. We turned in early. I needed to get busy on my book, so I went up to write. Being in my old room brought to me old memories of my dad and mom long ago. I remembered how happy I was when I had my first book published. I was so glad that I could come back to my old room. I have such great memories here.

The next morning, I got up a little earlier than normal. Mom was going out the door, off to do her whatevers. I decided to stay home and get some work done. Around lunchtime, the phone rang. It was Mom. "Angie, I need you to come and meet me at the diner. We need to talk."

I put up my work immediately and drove down to the diner. Mom was already there. I went over to the table and sat down. I knew immediately something was wrong. "What is it, Mom?" I asked.

"I have something to tell you. I want you to promise to stay calm."

"All right, Mom, what is it?"

"Well, I have not been feeling well lately. So I have been having some tests at the doctor's office and the hospital. The doctor asked me to have you come in with me this afternoon at three. He will give us the results."

"Oh, Mom, I hope there is nothing seriously wrong with you."

"Let's not get ahead of ourselves. We don't know what we are dealing with yet."

"Well, Mom, whatever it is, we are in this together."

We had our lunch, trying not to think of anything, and talked about small, trivial things to keep our mind off the major things. After lunch, we had about an hour. Since we could walk to the doctor's office, I suggested we walk around and browse some of the shops on the way.

It was time to walk on over to the doctor's office. We went in, and the nurse showed us to a sitting room. The doctor came in almost immediately. He was very solemn, so I knew it could not be good news. He sat at his desk and said, "I am sorry to say the news is not good. I had hoped it would not be bad news, but I am afraid the fact is you do have lung cancer. There are some things we can do. You can have some treatments. Hopefully you will go into remission for a while, but I am sorry to say there is no cure."

I don't think I even heard past the word *cancer*. I hate that word. He told Mom he would give her a day or two to think about what she wanted to do. "You can have some chemotherapy or some radiation. I need to know what you want to do. If you want to have treatments, I can give you something to boost your immune system before we start. It is up to you talk it over with your daughter and let me know what you want to do. Do you have any questions?"

We both said not at this time, then Mom said, "Well, doctor, if I do treatments or radiation, or both, will it make a difference?"

"What I hope it will do is put you into remission and give you more time. I cannot tell you how much time or the quality of your life."

"Thank you, doctor. I will call you."

We left the doctor's office. We were both numb. I felt bad Mom had to drive home herself, but I would be right behind her, and

THE CRYING WILLOWS

from now on I would be driving her. Maybe this was the reason I had waited so long to wear John's ring. One thing I knew was that I would stay with my mom as long as she needed me. I told her I would like to give up my apartment and come home; I would leave it up to her.

We talked that evening about everything, about her treatments, me coming home to live, about the house, about everything. Mom and I went over all the options the doctor had suggested. I told Mom it was totally up to her. I could not tell her what to do, but I would support her in any decision she made.

"I think I will go to my apartment for the rest of the week, pack things up, and give up my apartment. If that is all right with you."

"That is fine with me, if that is what you really want to do. I don't want you to quit living your life."

"I won't. John can come here to see me. We have our whole lives ahead of us. I want to know you are all right before I get married."

"All right, dear, go ahead and pack up this weekend. I want to talk to Pastor Whitmire and to your Aunt Cindy by myself. I will do those two things this weekend while you are packing up your apartment. Jack can help you move your things back to the house."

"I will go in the morning and should be through by the end of the week. Promise me if you need me you will call."

"I will, I promise, Angie."

CHAPTER 37

Going Home to Mom's House

I got my apartment packed up with the help of Jack. We finally got everything moved to the house. After Jack and I put all my boxes of things I did not need in the shed, Mom and I had dinner. We stayed in that night and just had a relaxing evening. On Sunday, we went to church. The service was very uplifting and just what I needed to hear. In the afternoon, Mom and I talked a long while. She told me she had decided to do treatments and anything else the doctor recommended. That was fine with me; it really was her decision.

She told me she had a doctor's appointment on Tuesday. I told her I would go with her. She agreed this time. I think Mom was a little scared, and who wouldn't be? But she was a strong lady and would never say that to anyone.

I chose to call John that night. We talked a long while. John's first question was "Are you wearing the ring?"

"Yes, John. I do love you."

"Does this mean you will marry me?"

"Yes, John, I will marry you. We must talk about some things. John, my mom is sick. She has lung cancer. I will have to stay with her and see her through."

"Of course, Angie, I understand. I can come there to see you, and when your mom is feeling all right, you can come here. We will work it out. I will wait for you, Angie, no matter how long it takes."

That is the man I was counting on. I got off the phone and relaxed for a little while. I was a little tired after having packed, cleaned, and moved my things in three days with the help of Jack. I chose not to write that night but told myself I had to get back to it tomorrow.

That night I tried to process everything that had happened the last week and tried to make sense of Mom's situation. I prayed that night and ask God to have His will; if it could be His will, please let my mom live.

The morning brought to us rain. I was hoping just for today so tomorrow we would have a good day to go to the doctor's appointment. I went down to check on Mom. Florence had breakfast ready. Mom was trying to eat. I had a bagel with cream cheese and some coffee and sat with Mom while she ate. I told her I was going to write for a while, and she should call if she needed me. She promised she would.

I would just be upstairs. Then it hit me. I probably should set up a place downstairs in the den. I would run that by Mom and would do that after the doctor's appointment tomorrow.

I came down and told Mom my idea about working downstairs. She also thought it was a good idea. We took a walk out into the garden and talked. She had a great attitude; that goes a long way for getting better. We knew we would have to take it one step at a time.

The next morning, Mom and I got up. I had my coffee, and she chose not to have anything. At the doctor's, she told him that she was ready to do whatever he thought would help. He suggested fifteen radiation treatments and maybe some chemo down the road. The radiation would sometimes put it into remission. She decided she would start as soon as possible. She started her treatments on Monday. The doctor prescribed something to build her immune system and gave her some supplements.

We settled into a routine: doctor's appointments, church on Sunday. We always enjoyed the services, and when we got home, we had a relaxing afternoon. She went every day for treatments. She did well for about four treatments. They then began to make her sick. She started another prescription for nausea. She finished her first round of radiation, and it did not prove as favorable as the doctor had hoped. He suggested chemotherapy for six treatments. She began to get very sick. The doctor decided she needed to rest before taking any more. He did some more tests and X-rays and called us in the next week.

When we got there, the nurse took us straight into his office. I knew the news could not be good when the doctor came in and sat down. He said exactly what we did not want to hear. He told us he did not think any more radiation or chemo would help. He suggested Mom just try to enjoy what time she had left. If the pain got too bad, he could make her comfortable. He said he would do more chemo if she wanted. Mom said no. We went straight home. Mom lay down. I fixed her favorite soup and made her some tea. When she got up, she did eat a little soup. She said she would have some hot tea before bed.

She said she wanted to ask something of me. I said, "Sure, what is it, Mom?" She wanted John and me to get married here.

"I want to attend my daughter's wedding."

"Oh, Mom, that is a great idea. I will talk to John tonight."

Before bed, I called John. He was very happy. He said he did not care where we got married as long as we did. I told him to ask Johnese and Danese to help and see if they all could fit it into their schedule the end of next month. It was set. I was excited but nervous. I did love John and wanted to marry him; it was very important for my mom to be part of my wedding.

That night, it hit me for the first time: my mom was dying. I cried for a long time. Then I knew I had to pull myself together for her.

The morning brought a beautiful day. I got up early and went for a ride on Ginger. When I returned home, I found out that Johnese had phoned. I called her back. She was so excited. She was talking a mile a minute. I finally calmed her down long enough to hear what she was saying. She wanted to design my dress. That was much more than I expected but all right.

I had a lot to do in a month. I knew it would be rushed but I could make it nice and what I wanted. John, Johnese, and Danese would be arriving on the second Tuesday of next month, and John and I would be married on Saturday.

When Mom got up, I fixed us some toast and coffee, and we had breakfast. I told her everything was arranged except what we would have to do here. I told her that Johnese was going to design my dress. That made Mom happy.

The entire time between now and the wedding would be busy. I just had to make sure Mom did not get too tired. We started making plans. I called the bakery and arranged a tasting for the next week. That would give them three weeks to make it. I thought while Mom and I were out we would also go by the florist and pick out my flowers.

I would call Andy and see if one of his girls would be my flower girl. I would call Pastor Whitmire, and everything would be set, except someone to give me away. After thinking about it, I thought Jack should be the one to give me away. I would tell John to pick his best man and the ring bearer. I wanted him to feel he was part of the wedding planning.

When the morning came, I waited late to go down. I asked Mom if she was able to go with me. She said she was; she was already dressed. I had my coffee and slipped into some jeans, and we were off to the bakery. Mom and I both tasted three cakes. She picked one, and I picked one, then we tasted both. We decided on the one I chose. It would be a three-tier cake, white inside, cream outside, with orange and yellow flowers and fall leaves. Next, we went to the florist and picked the flowers. Mom was better at that than me, so she picked the flowers for decorating. I picked my bouquet. We then went home. I was afraid Mom would get too tired.

When we went to church on Sunday, we talked to Pastor Whitmire, and he agreed to marry us. Our church pianist would play. We would decorate the church on Thursday before the wedding. Johnese would be here to help.

That evening, Mom called me to her room. She went over to her jewelry box and put something in my hand. It was a beautiful diamond necklace. I had never seen one like it and I had never seen my mother wear it, not that I could remember. She said, "This was my mother's necklace. I want you to have it. I would like you to wear it when you get married." I was so glad to have it; it was beautiful.

On Monday morning, we did not do anything. We rested most of the day. We knew the rest of the weeks before the wedding would be busy. About 3:00, Mom asked if we could go to our favorite little diner called Casey's. I said sure, so we went and sat in our same place and ate the same meal. I was glad my mom was eating a little bit. It was nice; just the two of us. I had a feeling I would always remember this meal.

On our way home, we talked about how much we enjoyed dinner and just about regular things. We really had not talked about anything else. I would leave that up to Mom.

When we got home, Mom went to bed early. I went to the den to write. I got up very early the next morning; everyone would be arriving that day. Mom and I had a quiet breakfast. Then I was off to the airport to pick everyone up. The flight was on time. I think it took as long to put the bags in the car as the flight took, or so it seemed. We got to the house, and we took the bags to their perspective rooms. Even though Danese had a great business sense, she was also a natural caregiver. As soon as she got to the house, she took over with Mom. I appreciated it, because right now it was badly needed.

Johnese was almost as excited about my dress as I was. She could not wait to show it to me. She really had outdone herself this time. It was the most beautiful dress I had ever seen. It had a scooped neckline with sheer tulle material on the arms and just above my neckline. My veil was made of tulle, and my dress was stitched with silver thread. It was form-fitting with a little split sleeve. It came to my ankle with a split on the side. It had beading on the bodice, around my hairline, and on the edge of my veil. We had to put it away now so John could not see it. I had tried it on; everything fit perfectly. We put it away and went down to check on Mom.

We decided to sit by the fire that night after dinner, which was delightful. Florence had outdone herself. She made a huge dinner and Mom's favorite soup. We had a great time talking by the fire. It had been a long day, so we retired to our respective rooms for the evening.

I lay in my bed that night thinking. I would be a married woman in four days; tomorrow would be Thursday, three days until my wedding. Johnese and I would decorate the church, then all that was left would be the ceremony. I wanted to get married, but I was nervous. I wanted to do it now so Mom could be there. Oh, how I missed my dad. I wished he could have been there; he would have been so proud. I was excited about my new life. Sleep finally came.

The morning brought in rain. Well, I could be thankful we were decorating inside. Johnese and I would have fun no matter what. I got up and dressed in jeans, a T-shirt, and a long-sleeved shirt on top. I went down to have some breakfast. That morning, we had cereal, toast, a fruit bowl, and yogurt. My kind of breakfast. Johnese and I went to decorate the church. We stopped at the florist and picked up the flowers, candles, and everything we needed. We went to the church and started decorating. We started with the candles. Once they were in place, we placed the flowers around. We kept changing things; we would try it here, then try it there, until finally it was in the perfect spot.

When we finished four hours later, I thought we had done a great job. The church looked beautiful. I looked at the chapel. The thought hit me that the next time I see it, I would be walking down the aisle. The thought made me a little nervous, a little excited, and a little anxious.

My bridesmaids' dresses were sage green with fall colors around the neckline and the waist. They were sewn with silver thread and were form-fitting. Mom and Aunt Cindy's dresses were also sage green, sewn with silver thread.

When we got home, Mom and Danese had been having a good time. John was in the library. He asked what we wanted to do for dinner. Mom wanted to stay home, so we ordered from our favorite little diner in town. John and I went to pick up dinner. I told John I was the luckiest woman in the world to be getting a husband who did not mind his wife having to stay with her mom. John told me he loved me and wanted me to be happy. He knew I would want to stay with my mom. Then he said, "Are you nervous?"

"A little. What about you?"

"Well, yes, a little. One and a half days. Not backing out, are you, Angie?"

"Oh no. You?"

"No, never."

The morning of the wedding finally arrived. We were all turning in every direction, it seemed. Finally everything ready except me. I took my dress and went over to the fellowship hall and dressed.

Johnese was with me. Danese was making sure the flowers girls were ready and doing the lineup for me, the ring bearer and all that. In a moment, a knock came at my door. It was time. I took one more look in the mirror. I couldn't believe my eyes. Johnese had outdone herself once again.

My mom and Aunt Cindy were escorted down the aisle. The flower girls were scattering petals here and there, then the ring bearer, then the bridesmaids and their escorts. Then the "Wedding March" began to play. Jack took my arm and escorted me down the aisle. All I could think of was how much I missed my dad, and how proud he would be of me. Then I saw John standing there so handsome, and I just thought, *This is it.* He was the only one I could ever want. He looked so handsome standing at the altar. His expression let me know I looked great too. When the wedding vows ended, we kissed outside. I threw my bouquet. Johnese caught it. John and I left in the car, realizing we had not made any plans past the wedding.

We went back to Mom's house. She was still on cloud nine. She looked beautiful. We took lots and lots of pictures, talked and talked, ate and ate. Mom was just elated that she had gotten to attend my wedding. John and I went upstairs to talk and decide what to do. John said he really needed to get back, so my wedding night was spent in my old room. Not quite the way I had dreamed it. That did not make it any less special. John would have to leave the next day but promised that when I came back to Virginia for good, he would let me plan a honeymoon, any one I wanted; so we agreed.

That night was wonderful with John. I was sorry he had to leave but I had no regrets about staying. The morning came, bringing us wonderful weather. John, Johnese, and Danese were finally ready to go, so I drove them to the airport. It was hard to see them go, especially John, but I knew it was the right thing.

As I drove back to the house, I was happy and sad; my emotions were a mess. I just couldn't stop looking at my rings. I was married.

When I got home, Mom was resting. I left her alone. I knew she must be worn out. I put away all the food, and Florence and I cleaned up. She had fixed Mom some soup. I told her I did not want anything just yet. We sat and talked. Florence was such a good person. Jack came by and brought me a new saddle for Ginger. I told him I would try it tomorrow.

I offered Jack food, and he took it. We were all in the dining room when Mom came down. She sat with us and had her soup. I had a salad and some bread sticks and, of course, my coffee.

John and I talked on the phone every night, and he FaceTimed me almost every day. Johnese called at least once a week. She always updated me on Janese. I had sent her a present back with Johnese. She said Janese loved it. Mom was looking tired the next morning. I asked if there was anything; she said no. We always went to the garden to sit but it was getting cold now. We decided that our tea would have to be by the fire these days. Mom rarely went out anymore. She was feeling much worse. I knew, but she never complained. We still went to church on Sunday morning. That was the only time she got out. I went out to do the shopping we needed, and I always took her to the doctor.

Thanksgiving was coming up. John and Johnese were coming. Danese had to stay to take care of business and check on Janese. We did not do a lot for Thanksgiving; just a big meal.

For Thanksgiving, there would be a few more people. Mom and myself, of course, and Jack and Florence as usual. John and Johnese would arrive on Wednesday night and leave on Sunday night.

Four days with John seemed heavenly to me. We had a wonderful meal on Thursday. Sunday came much too soon. Our days were mostly just staying in. I was getting a lot done on my book. I had gotten used to writing in the den. Mom and I still had our talks and tea in front of the fireplace.

On Wednesday, John and Johnese arrived, and I picked them up at the airport. This visit was an unscheduled one, but it turned out to be a great one. John thought I needed a break, so he and Johnese came to give me one, and they did. Johnese stayed with Mom while John and I went out for the evening. It was nice to go out for a change. Sunday evening arrived much too soon. Johnese said she had enjoyed her stay and that she had gotten a lot of work done. I said goodbye once again. I was always torn when he left. It had been marvelous to have a few days. I loved my Mom dearly and definitely knew I was doing the right thing, but I did miss John so much.

We would start getting ready for Christmas now that Thanksgiving was over. Florence and Jack helped me and Mom. Mom loved Christmas. Mom and I always took a drive to see the lights. We also used to go to the Christmas parade. I did not think Mom was able this year. We would wait and see. I read the newspaper to her. I told her the parade was on Saturday. She said she did not think she could do that this year but that she would still like to take our drive to see the lights. We planned to do that any night she felt strong enough.

Jack, Florence, and I finished decorating the house, and Jack decorated outside. The tree in the house was gorgeous this year, and Jack had really worked hard on the outside. All the trees were decorated. The deer were up with their lights on, and the snowman that Mom liked so much. The wreaths were lighted on the door and on either side of the house. It looked beautiful. Florence and I put a few extra touches in each room of the house.

The next evening, Mom was feeling strong enough, so we took our drive. I made sure she was wrapped up warm, and we took our drive to see the lights. They were very impressive this year. Lots of them, and very well done. I felt like a little girl again. I always did when we went to see the lights. It just always reminded me of those days as a child when Mom and Dad would take me to see the lights. We came back and drank hot chocolate by the fire.

Mom slept late the next morning. I figured she was tired. When she got up, I had breakfast with her. I hated to see Mom give up all her community projects. She could still get up and walk around. I was thankful for that and for every day we had together. We made hot chocolate and apple cider and handed it out to carolers that came by each evening. I made Christmas cookies; they smelled and looked wonderful.

This was such a nice season, the most special to me. I went shopping for everyone. I bought John a suit and Johnese her favorite perfume and a briefcase I had seen Danese admiring when she was here. I shopped for everyone except Mom. What could I get her? I had gotten her some slippers, a book, a soft warm robe, and a fuzzy throw for the bed, but I wanted something special for her. I ended up at the jewelry store. I suppose because I always got her jewelry.

I looked and looked. I saw a locket. It was a beautiful silver locket. I had my name and hers engraved on it. It was a double locket for two pictures. I would put one of her and one of me in it. I also got something for Aunt Cindy at the jewelry store.

When I got home, I checked on Mom. She was feeling all right. I asked if she felt like letting me take a picture of her this evening by the fireplace. She said yes. I took a picture of Mom, and had Florence take a picture of me, then both of us together. The next day, I had our pictures put into the locket and I had the one of the two of us put into an eight-by-ten picture frame so I would have one to hang on my wall in my new home.

When I returned that evening, Florence wanted me to talk with Mom. She was insisting on a real tree this year. I just told Florence that this meant we would be decorating the tree all over again. I called Jack and asked if he would get a real tree for the house, and he did. I knew this was important to her, so Jack and I went shopping for a real tree.

We settled on a beautiful fir tree. It was seven feet tall and had a wonderful shape for a real tree. This reminded me of Christmas as a child. We always had a real tree. My dad and I would always go and select the tree. We got it home and began to decorate all the lights from years past, all the decorations with special meanings only to us. It was such fun. Florence always had a knack for Christmas trees. Jack finished lighting up the drive and the walkway. We wrapped up and went out to see what a marvelous job Jack had done once again. It was unbelievable.

Mom so enjoyed this. I guess this is where my love of Christmas came from. When we went back into the house, we had some hot apple cider and sat by the fire.

Now that the decorating was done, I got back to my book. I worked hard the next week to get as much done as I could before the hullabaloo of Christmas took over. I called Andy to make sure he was bringing his family. Kids always made me happy at Christmas. It just was not the same without kids.

I told Mom the next morning I wanted to make her a doctor's appointment. She said she wanted to wait until after Christmas.

I went shopping for last-minute things. I bought extra tape and wrapping paper. I could always put it up for next year. Then I went in search of the ornament. We always bought a new ornament each year. I went to the Christmas Shop for my new ornament. I did what Mom always did. I walked around looking at all the ornaments until one caught my eye. I bought it and had it wrapped so Mom could open it. When I got home, I put all the presents under the tree except the ornament.

I took it up to my room. When dinner was over, I went with Mom to the sitting room and told her I would be right back. I went and got the ornament and brought it to Mom to unwrap. She loved it. She walked over to the tree and found the perfect spot and hung it there. I mentally marked the branch that it hung on. That is where it would always hang, not just on that tree but on whatever tree I had.

It was becoming more real to me each day that Mom was getting much worse. There was a homeless shelter we volunteered at during the season, so Jack and I went two nights that week. It was very rewarding.

I was getting excited about Christmas. Our Christmas play was tonight at church. Mom did not feel like going, so Jack and I went, and Florence stayed with Mom.

John and Johnese would be in tonight. I would pick them up at 10:00 p.m. I was excited to see them. Their flight was on time. We collected their luggage and headed home. John looked so good to me. Johnese, of course, was her upbeat self. I knew she would bring life into the house.

We talked about Janese. She sent me something for Christmas. I had gotten her a large doll so that she could dress it in her clothes. Johnese said that Janese's line was doing well. Thursday evening, John and I took a carriage ride. It was so fun. As we were coming back to his house, it was just beginning to snow. It was wonderful. Friday and Saturday, we spent every moment together that we could, then we opened our gifts after dinner on Saturday. We always saved one gift for Christmas Day. We got up early Christmas morning and opened our one gift; usually it was the best one.

THE CRYING WILLOWS

The snow had stopped on Friday but came back on Saturday. John and I took a walk in the snow. I loved walking in the snow. We saw a fox running through the field as we walked back to the house.

I had also gotten Johnese a pair of earrings, and Mom her locket. Andy and his family would stop by on Christmas Day, and Aunt Cindy had already been. I bought John a new smartphone. Obviously, John had been talking to Mom; he bought me a ring. I suppose the cat was out of the bag. Now he knew if he bought me rings and shoes, it would always be fine.

I enjoyed this holiday, but it ended much too soon. I took John and Johnese back to the airport. Johnese had a time getting that doll on the plane; that is one we could talk about in the coming years. I said goodbye to John. We so wanted to be together but the time was not yet, and I was also glad for that. It sometimes seems to be a hard spot to be in, but it is really not. Although I love John and want to be with him, I also love Mom and don't want her to die. The thought of losing her just hurts so badly.

CHAPTER 38

Taking Care of Mom

I left John and Johnese getting on the plane. I always had mixed feelings at these times. I would still call John every night and talk to Johnese once a week. I knew Mom really needed me now. She was getting much worse. The days ahead would be getting colder, so I ask Jack to make sure our house was winterized properly, and I turned up the heat a little upstairs.

I asked Mom in the morning if she would make a doctor's appointment, and she agreed to make one for one day this week. I asked her if she wanted me to take down the Christmas decorations. She said no, not just yet. I didn't care but thought it strange. She usually wanted it down as soon as Christmas was over.

We had nice talks in front of the fire. She slept in the den on the day bed, and I slept on the couch in the den to be close to her. The doctor's office called with an appointment on Thursday. Upon arriving, the doctor came out and escorted mom into a room. She never wanted me to go in with her, and she did not this time either. I sat waiting in the lobby. Finally, the doctor came out and talked to me. He told me Mom would now need round-the-clock care. He would be starting her on morphine. I assured him I would be able to be there all the time and I did have a backup if need be.

He said he would offer any assistance he could and that he would send a nurse once a week. I thanked him. He said he would send Mom out now. Although I wanted to run away and scream, I got my composure and waited for Mom to come through the door. I waited until she was through at the checkout window. As we walked to the car, I told her I would pick up her medicine on the way home if she felt like waiting. She said yes, that would be fine. Then she said, "I'm dying, you know."

"Yes, Mom, I know, and you don't have to worry. I will be with you as long as you need me to be."

That was all she said about it, then she said, "Let's go to our diner before we go home."

"Sure, Mom, whatever you want." I went to the drugstore and picked up her meds. Her morphine was in pill form for now. We were off to Casey's diner. It was like old times for a few moments. We ordered whatever we wanted plus dessert. After dinner, we went home. I knew Mom was tired. I helped her to the den. We talked about her new meds. She said she would start them tomorrow. We sat by the fire for a while, then she went to bed.

I went up to my old room for a while to write. I sometimes felt I might be disturbing her. She always told me I was not, but I knew my Mom; she never complained about anything. I said a prayer before I went back down. I knew the days ahead were not going to be easy. None of us are strong enough to handle these kinds of things by ourselves. I just asked the Lord for strength to get me through and for strength for my mom. By the time I came back down, Mom was asleep.

I went on to bed and had a very restless night.

The morning brought our first big snowstorm. We'd had snow but nothing of much concern. We had four inches. When we woke up, we got snow off and on during the day. By the evening, we had six inches. It was beautiful and not terribly bad. We could still get out if need be. We, of course, would stay in. Florence was already here. She always stayed over if it snowed, and Jack lived close enough to walk if he needed to.

I didn't worry too much; we would be fine. I had just gotten groceries the day before the storm, so we were good. I would for sure be sitting in front of the fire this evening. I loved the snow as much as I liked to take a ride on Ginger. She liked the snow as much as I did, so I took a short ride in the snow.

After we had dinner, we went into the great room, sat by the fire, and talked over some hot chocolate. We always did this time of evening. Mom asked if could we go to the garden tomorrow. I told her we would if the snow was gone and the temperature was right.

The morning brought to us sunshine. I was happy. I wanted to take Mom to the garden. I told Mom we would go to the garden in the afternoon. I bundled her up, and we walked out to the garden and sat on the bench for a while. The morphine had stopped her pain and had not affected her body yet. Mom loved her garden. It was 4:30, so we went inside. We went to the great room and sat by the fire. We talked until dinner.

John was coming today. He would only be here for the weekend. It always excited me when he came, even if just for a couple of days. He told me that he would be getting a car. He did not want me to drive in this weather even though it never bothered me to drive in the snow.

He arrived about 10:00 on Friday evening. We had a great time. Aunt Cindy came over to spend some time with Mom, so John and I went out for the day. We took in a movie and went to all the antique shops and had lunch. Aunt Cindy was still there when we arrived back at the house. She was always fun and entertaining. Aunt Cindy said goodbye and we put a net flick on for all of us to watch. Mom had had a great day and so had we.

On Sunday, John and I decided we would stay at home with Mom. She had gotten so she could not go to church anymore. I usually went, but Mom just didn't feel good and was very tired. After breakfast was over, we all went into the great room and sat by the fire. All of us, John, Jack, Florence, myself, and Mom, had a wonderful morning talking about the past and about things we had enjoyed over the years. We talked about my dad, the horses, and, of course, Florence. I thought she came with the house. Turns out my dad had hired Florence and built her a house on the property before I was born. Dad had wanted horses but did not know much about them, so when Jack moved down the road, Dad hired him to buy and take care of our horses.

Florence got up to fix lunch. Jack needed to go home. John's flight would not be until 8:00 p.m., so he could have dinner with us. Florence made Mom some soup, and John and I skipped lunch and took a long walk. We had dinner at 6:00. Mom just had soup.

She was beginning to have trouble keeping down food. Florence had fixed a lovely meal, after which John and I took a walk in the garden. We talked about Mom and sat there just enjoying our time together. We went back. John told Mom goodbye, then he had to leave for the airport. I really hated to see him go.

Mom was getting worse. I knew it, and so did John. We really did not talk about it, though. He kissed me goodbye and said, "I love you. If you need me, call." I promised I would.

CHAPTER 39

A Farewell to Mom

I knew in the coming days we were going to have to have a talk about things. I just did not know how to do it.

The next morning, Mom asked me to talk with her, so we went to the great room in front of the fireplace where we had always had our talks, good ones, bad ones, happy and sad ones. She started by saying, "Angie, we can't put this off any longer. I want you to be with we when Martin comes today. We have much to discuss and I need to do it with you." Martin was her lawyer.

"Oh, Mom, I am glad. I did not know how to bring up the subject."

"He will be here after lunch today. We will get things taken care of now." She handed me a box and said, "I want you to take this box to your room. When the time comes, it has everything in it you will need to know. All my funeral arrangements are in it, even to the dress I shall wear, the songs to be sung, and who to sing them. Our pastor, of course, will do the service. The names of the pallbearers are in there."

"I hate talking about this, Mom, but thank you for being such an amazing mom and thank you for arranging things the way you have, the way you want them."

"I'm so proud you, Angie, and all your accomplishments."

"It is because I had you for a mom."

"Don't open the box. Just yet wait until you need to. We will go over my will with you today."

I took the box to my room, hoping I would not have to open it any time soon. We had some lunch, and just about the time we finished, the doorbell rang. It was Martin. We went into the great room and sat down. "Angie, your mom came to me two years ago and made out her will. I will go over it with you now. If there is anything you don't understand, let me know and we will explain."

"All right, I will." I was thinking it should be pretty cut and dried; I was an only child.

Martin started to read. He read about the house. It was mine, of course. Mom had left Florence a good severance pay package, and she could live in the house she was staying in until death. Any money, CDs, things of that nature, would go to me. Ginger would be mine, but all the other horses would go to Jack. I thought that was fair. Mom also left a few pieces in the house to Florence. And I would be in charge of the Larrimore Foundation. It seems that it was founded by my dad in honor of Trent Larrimore. I did not know Trent Larrimore. I did not understand. He was my dad's brother, my uncle. Mom spoke up and said there would be more of an explanation in the box.

I expected the foundation would still need to be kept up, but by me? I had no experience with fundraising or community affairs. I suppose one could learn anything.

We all agreed and signed the will. Martin left. Mom was really tired. I helped her to bed. I knew it would not be too long. She could hardly get up anymore. I'm glad the will was signed and that was over. I dreaded that. I just never wanted to think about things like that, but it had to be done.

Time went very slowly during the month of January. I stayed with Mom most of the time. I was thankful for Florence; she helped me so much. She did most of the grocery shopping now. I cleaned and helped her cook, and I cared for Mom all the time. Jack also went above his duties. He made sure all the outside work was done. He was so good to make sure the horses were cared for. It made things so much easier for me. Aunt Cindy was coming the next day. I might go out; I usually did.

Cindy arrived. She came in trying to cheer up Mom. Mom now was so weak she could hardly speak. Cindy was not ready to see Mom that way. I decided not to go out today; I just wanted to stay and talk with Aunt Cindy. We visited awhile while Mom was sleeping. When she got ready to leave, she told me to call her anytime I needed her.

The next day was a particularly bad day for Mom. John called as he always did that evening. He asked what was wrong. I told him Mom had had a really bad day. He asked if he should come; I told him no, but he said he was coming anyway. He came in that evening. The next day, Mom was sick. During the last year, I had done everything possible to find something that would help. I planted vegetables in the greenhouse; we grew them organically. I bought every herb and anything that said would help, but nothing had. She was in a real bad way, so I called the doctor.

He came out to the house and stayed about an hour. He told me and John it would probably be just a matter of hours. Mom called for me. She asked me to move her to the window so she could see the garden.

Mom's voice was so weak. She told me she loved me. I told her I loved her too. John and I moved her hospital bed over to the window. I sat with her, and we looked at the garden together. I was afraid she would get cold, so I got some more cover for her bed. We sat by the window for a long while. She drifted off to sleep.

The morning brought a cold but beautiful day. The sun was out. Mom got down a few bites of soup this morning. I sat with her. We looked at the garden together. I started talking to her about the garden and the things we did there as a child. She smiled, closed her eyes, and stopped breathing. She was gone. I knew it but I did not want to hear it.

The doctor had come in just before she died. He called the funeral home. They came and took her away. I broke down. I was so thankful that John had come. The pastor was there by lunchtime, bringing food. John and I had to go to the funeral home to make arrangements.

I called Aunt Cindy and Andy. I dreaded the next few days. I felt a deep loss, a loneliness I had not felt since my dad died. I was so thankful I had married John.

Florence was cleaning. Jack was caring for the house. John and I went on to the funeral home. Aunt Cindy stayed at the house with

Florence and Jack to receive friends and family. The funeral home's receiving of friends would be tomorrow night and the funeral on Friday. Johnese and Danese would arrive on Thursday afternoon.

We got through the viewing. The pastor was so helpful. It seems as though while I was away Mom was planning her funeral. That was so like her. She left out no details. I looked through the box. The pastor already knew what she wanted; he also had a copy of the arrangements. My mom; that was who she was, never complaining, never talking about herself, always helping someone else.

The funeral was over, and we went back to the house. Everyone was there. When everyone finally left, I went to Mom's room and sat on her bed for a while. I don't know, I just felt close to her there. This entire time had felt like an unreal dream, one I could not wake from.

I would have to stay here for a couple of weeks to go over the will and decide on some things. So I told John I would be home in a couple of weeks.

Johnese and Danese were such a big help. They helped Florence, and I could not have made it through without John and the Lord. I told them goodbye. When they were all gone, it hit me. My mom was gone forever. I cried a long while, then tried to rest a bit. I finally made myself get up.

Florence was there, cooking dinner as always.

The next morning, I started packing up the house. The more I thought about it, the more I did not want to. I decided I would just pack up the things that were special to me, such as Mom's china, her jewelry, pictures. That was all I wanted right now. I thought about leaving the house. It was hard to think about the house just sitting there. I could never sell it. What could I do?

Jack was moving the horses but was still caring for Ginger. I asked him to take all the cats except Tabitha. I would have to sleep on all this. I really did not know what to do.

The next morning, I happened to remember Florence did not own her house. She had just always lived there. My dad had that house built on our property so that Florence would be close by. Maybe we could work something out.

Florence was coming today to help me. When she arrived, I asked her to sit and talk with me. We sat down. I know she was wondering why I wanted to talk with her.

"Florence, I want to ask a favor of you. If you are not interested, just say no. I want to know if you would be willing to move in here and take care of this place. I can't just leave it with no one in it. I need you, Florence, I have always needed you. You have always been like family to me. If you would do this, I would only want to come in from time to time. I would always let you know. It would be your house the rest of the time. When we come in, you could stay in the house."

"I will think about it and let you know tomorrow."

Florence and I packed up the things I wanted to take. When we were finished and she was ready to leave, she said, "I'll see you in the morning." I had already gone over the will with both her and Jack. She knew they had a severance package. Jack came by every day to see if we needed anything.

I went to Mom's and my favorite diner in town. I sat there missing her so badly but enjoying the food and atmosphere as we always did. I went home and got ready for bed. I called John and told him goodnight and told him I would try to come to the estate by the end of next week.

I put all my thoughts aside and went to sleep. The morning brought some snow showers. It snowed off and on all day. Florence came about 10:30. We had breakfast together. I cooked for a change. We talked about Mom and the house and how eating breakfast together was a great memory for me. "In the summer, when Mom worked and Dad was gone, you and I always ate breakfast together."

She told me she had decided to take me up on my offer. I said we will have to work out the details. "If you agree with this, I think we will both win. If anything major happens to the house. I will take care of it. You would be responsible for small things, and I would to pay the taxes and insurance. We could employ Jack together. I will pay half his salary, and you pay half. You are free to rent the house you currently live in, and with that money and your social security, you should be able to manage well." She said she had already made up her mind; she agreed.

"Florence, you have taken a load off my mind." I called Jack. He agreed to do the yard work, maintenance, and care of Ginger. All that was left now was to find about this foundation and what was expected of me, then I could go to the estate.

Florence had already rented out the rest of the horse stables and her house so she would have money for repairs and her part of Jack's salary. The severance package would pay the taxes and insurance for probably as long as she would need it. I told her if she ever got into trouble to call me. I would be finishing up here by the end of next week. "Thank you, Florence. You don't know what this means to me. Mom would be happy."

CHAPTER 40

The Willows Call

The Larrimore foundation was not too bad. I didn't need to do a lot, just a fundraiser once a year, a speech at their dinner twice a year, and, of course, keep up with what was happening.

The foundation was to fund homes for runaway children. There was a story behind this. It seems as though my uncle Trent went away to work in a large city. He found a boy on the streets and took him in. He then founded this foundation. When he died, my dad wanted to continue his work. So now it is my turn.

Everything was done. I now could leave. It would be hard; thanks to Florence and Jack, not as hard as it would have been. At the same time, I felt excited to be going home back to the estate. It was as if the willows were calling me. I was a new bride. That scared me a little. I had not lived with John, so it would be different. I knew I would be happy, though. When I called John to tell him I would be coming to the estate the next day, he was very happy. He said he would pick me up at the airport.

The morning came too soon. I got up and dressed. Florence was in the kitchen cooking breakfast for me. She had already started moving in. I thanked her again and had breakfast with her. I then had to get ready to leave. I took a few moments and looked at each room, thinking of how things were as a child and the things Mom and I did. The great room was the hardest of all. We had great talks there. I really would miss her. I called Jack before I left to tell him I was leaving. Then I called Andy to tell him I would allow him to see some of my new book as soon as possible.

When I got to the airport, John was waiting for me. He gathered my luggage, and we were off to the estate. He gave me a kiss when we were in the car. He told me he was sorry about Mom but he was glad I was home. *Home*, I thought. that has a nice ring to it.

He had a surprise for me when we got to the estate. He parked the car in front of the house. We got out of the car, and when we got to the door, he carried me across the threshold. I was surprised. That was not all. When we were inside, everyone was waiting. They had a party planned. This was very sweet. I was very tired but figured I could make it a little while longer.

It was a great party, just family and good food. We played games and sat in front of the fireplace talking until late. We went up to bed. I almost went to my old room. Then it hit me. John's room was now our room. The only difference was John's room was a lot larger and the balcony a lot larger too. I could see and hear the willows very clearly from here. My last surprise was brochures from all over the world. I was supposed to pick a honeymoon spot. I would do that tomorrow.

John's and my life together was just beginning. I felt very happy about it. I loved John and he loved me. My mom's life was over and that made me very sad. I would miss her terribly. I knew I would think of her every day. My life would be different now but happy.

Johnese had accepted me so readily, it pleased me that I fit in to this family so well.

I would go to see Janese tomorrow and tell her I would be coming to see her more often.

This night was special. John was such a thoughtful man. I was sure there would be many such nights ahead. There would be movies, picnics, theater, all the things we both loved, and, of course, my books.

I knew that John and I would have a good life. God always gives you what you need if we ask and believe. I am embarking on a new journey. I will be able to spend the rest of my life listening to the crying willows.

The End

ABOUT THE AUTHOR

Mason Lakey was raised in the Appalachian Mountains, in a unique culture where faith is strong and morals and character are important. Her hobbies include crocheting, painting, gardening, canning, cooking, reading, and—of course—writing. The author now resides in the country, in the Smoky Mountains. She loves her life.